Czech, Moravian and Slovak Fairy Tales

Czech, Moravian and Slovak Fairy Tales

Retold by
Parker Fillmore

With illustrations and decorations
by **Jan Matulka**

Hippocrene Books, Inc.
New York

𝕿𝖔

MISS MARJORIE RAHLSON

This edition © 1998 by Hippocrene Books, Inc.

Originally published in 1919 by
W. Collins Sons & Co., Ltd, London.

For information, address:
HIPPOCRENE BOOKS
171 Madison Avenue
New York, NY 10016

*Cataloging-in-Publication Data available from
the Library of Congress.*

ISBN 0-7818-0714-X

Printed in the United States of America.

NOTE

THIS rendering of some of the old Czechoslovak tales is not offered as a literal translation or a scholarly translation. I have retold the stories in a way that I hope will please American children. I have tried hard to keep the flavor of the originals but have taken the liberty of a short cut here and an elaboration there wherever these have seemed to me to make the English version clearer and more interesting.

I have gone to Czech, Slovakian, and Moravian sources. All these stories appear in many versions in the different folklore collections made by such native writers as Erben, Nemcova, Dobsinsky, Rimavsky, Benes-Trebizsky, Kulda. They represent the folk-tale in all stages of its development from the bald narrative of *The Bird with the Golden Gizzard* which Kulda reports with phonographic exactness, to Nemcova's more elaborate tale, *Prince Bayaya,* which is really a mosaic of two or three simpler stories. I have included *Katcha and the Devil* for the sake of its keen humor, which is particularly Czech in character; *The Betrothal Gifts* to show how a story common to other countries is made most charmingly local by giving it a local

NOTE

background; *The Three Golden Hairs* to contrast it with a famous German variant which it seems to me is much inferior to the Slavic version; and several fine stories of the prince gone off on adventures which in common with the folk-tales of all Europe show a strong Oriental influence.

In the transliteration of proper names I have not followed consistently any one method, but for each individual name have made what seemed to be the best selection from the various possible spellings. Until transliteration from the Slavic languages has become standardized this, I am sure, is permissible and even advisable.

In the preparation of this volume I have made heavy draughts upon the scholarship and patience of my Czech friends, Mrs. Jan Matulka and Mr. Vladimir Jelinek. I beg them to accept my thanks. I am also deeply grateful to Mr. A. B. Koukol, who did me the favor of reading the final sheets. Lastly I wish to express my appreciation of the Webster Branch of the New York Public Library, which has gathered together what is probably the most complete collection of Czechoslovak literature in America, and one particularly rich in folklore and children's books.

August, 1919

P. F.

CONTENTS

CONTENTS

FULL-PAGE ILLUSTRATIONS

LONGSHANKS, GIRTH, AND KEEN

THE STORY OF THREE WONDERFUL SERVING MEN

LONGSHANKS, GIRTH, AND KEEN

THERE was once an aged king who had an only son. One day he called the prince to him and said: "My dear son, you know that ripe fruit falls in order to make room for other fruit. This my old head is like ripe fruit and soon the sun will no longer shine upon it. Now before I die I should like to see you happily married. Get you a wife, my son."

"I would, my father, that I could please you in this," the prince answered, "but I know of no one who would make you a worthy daughter-in-law."

The old king reached into his pocket, drew out a golden key, and handed it to the prince. He said:

"Go up into the tower to the very top. There look about you and when you have decided what you like best of all you see, come back and tell me."

The prince took the key and at once mounted the tower. He had never before gone to the very top and he had never heard what was there. He went up and up until at last he saw a small iron door in the ceiling. He opened this with the golden key, pushed it back, and entered a large circular hall. The ceiling was blue and silver like the heavens on a bright night when the stars shine, and the floor was covered with a green silken carpet. There were twelve tall windows set in gold frames, and on the crystal glass of each window a beautiful young girl was pictured in glowing colors. Every one of them was a princess with a royal crown upon her head. As the prince looked at them it seemed to him that each was more lovely than the last, and for the life of him he knew not which was the loveliest. Then they began to move as if alive, and they smiled at the prince and nodded, and looked as if they were about to speak.

Suddenly the prince noticed that one of the twelve windows was covered with a white curtain. He pulled the curtain aside and there without any question was the most beautiful princess of them all, clothed in pure white, with a silver girdle and a crown of pearls. Her face was deathly pale and sad as the grave.

For a long time the prince stood before this picture in utter amazement and as he looked at it a pain seemed to enter his heart.

"This one I want for my bride," he said aloud, "this one and no other."

At these words the maiden bowed, flushed like a rose, and then instantly all the pictures disappeared.

When the prince told his father what he had seen and which maiden he had chosen, the old king was greatly troubled.

"My son," he said, "you did ill to uncover what was covered and in declaring this, your choice, you have exposed yourself to a great danger. This maiden is in the power of a black magician who holds her captive in an iron castle. Of all who have gone to rescue her not one has ever returned. However, what's done is done and you have given your word. Go, then, try what fortune has in store for you, and may Heaven bring you back safe and sound."

So the prince bade his father farewell, mounted his horse, and rode forth to find his bride. His first adventure was to lose his way in a deep forest. He wandered about some time not knowing where to turn when suddenly he was hailed from behind with these words:

"Hey, there, master, wait a minute!"

He looked around and saw a tall man running toward him.

"Take me into your service, master," the tall man said. "If you do you won't regret it."

"What is your name," the prince asked, "and what can you do?"

"People call me Longshanks because I can stretch myself out. I'll show you. Do you see a bird's nest in the top of that tall fir? I'll get it down for you and not by climbing the tree either."

So saying he began to stretch out and his body shot up and up until he was as tall as the fir tree. He reached over and got the nest and then, in a shorter time than it had taken him to stretch out, he reduced himself to his natural size.

"You do your trick very well," the prince said, "but just now a bird's nest isn't of much use to me. What I need is some one to show me the way out of this forest."

"H'm," Longshanks said, "that's an easy enough matter."

Again he began to stretch himself up and up and up until he was three times as tall as the highest pine in the forest. He looked around and said: "Over there, in that direction, is the nearest way out."

Then he made himself small again, took the horse by the bridle, walked ahead, and in a short time they emerged from the forest.

A broad plain stretched out before them and beyond it they could see tall gray rocks that looked like the walls of a great city and mountains overgrown with forests.

Longshanks pointed off across the plain and said: "There, master, goes a comrade of mine who would be very useful to you. You ought to take him into your service too."

"Very well," said the prince, "call him here that I may find out what sort of a fellow he is."

"He is too far away to call," Longshanks said. "He wouldn't hear my voice and if he did he would be a long time in reaching us, for he has much to carry. I had better step over and get him myself."

As he said this, Longshanks stretched out and out until his head was lost in the clouds. He took two or three strides, reached his comrade, set him on his shoulder, and brought him to the prince.

The new man was heavily built and round as a barrel.

"Who are you?" the prince asked. "And what can you do?"

"I am called Girth," the man said. "I can widen myself."

"Let me see you do it," the prince said.

"Very well, master," said Girth, beginning to puff

out, " I will. But take care! Ride off into the forest as fast as you can! "

The prince did not understand the warning, but he saw that Longshanks was in full flight, so he spurred his horse and galloped after him.

It was just as well he did, for in another moment Girth would have crushed both him and his horse, so fast did he spread out, so huge did he become. In a short time he filled the whole plain until it looked as though a mountain had fallen upon it.

When the plain was entirely covered, he stopped expanding, heaved a deep breath that shook the forest trees, and returned to his natural size.

" You made me run for my life! " the prince said. " I tell you I don't meet a fellow like you every day! By all means join me."

They went across the plain and as they neared the rocks they met a man whose eyes were bandaged with a handkerchief.

" Master," said Longshanks, " there is my other comrade. Take him into your service, too, and I can tell you you won't regret the bread he eats."

" Who are you? " the prince asked. " And why do you keep your eyes bandaged? You can't see where you're going."

" On the contrary, master, it is just because I see too well that I have to bandage my eyes. With bandaged eyes I see as well as other people whose eyes are uncovered. When I take the handkerchief off, my sight is so keen it goes straight through everything. When I look at anything intently it catches fire, and if it can't burn, it crumbles to pieces. On account of my sight I'm called Keen."

He untied the handkerchief, turned to one of the rocks opposite, and gazed at it with glowing eyes. Soon the rock began to crumble and fall to pieces. In a few moments it was reduced to a heap of sand. In the sand something gleamed like fire. Keen picked it up and handed it to the prince. It was a lump of pure gold.

" Ha, ha! " said the prince. " You are a fine fellow and worth more than wages! I should be a fool not to take you into my service. Since you have such keen eyes, look and tell me how much farther it is to the Iron Castle and what is happening there now."

" If you rode there alone," Keen answered, " you might get there within a year, but with us to help you, you will arrive this very day. Our coming is not unexpected, either, for at this very moment they are preparing supper for us."

"What is the captive princess doing?"

"She is sitting on a high tower behind an iron grating. The magician stands on guard."

"If you are real men," the prince cried, "you will all help me to free her."

The three comrades promised they would.

They led the prince straight through the gray rocks by a defile which Keen made with his eyes, and on and on through high mountains and deep forests. Whatever obstacle was in the way one or another of the three comrades was able to remove it.

By late afternoon they had crossed the last mountain, had left behind them the last stretch of dark forest, and they saw looming up ahead of them the Iron Castle.

Just as the sun sank the prince and his followers crossed the drawbridge and entered the courtyard gate. Instantly the drawbridge lifted and the gate clanged shut.

They went through the courtyard and the prince put his horse in the stable, where he found a place all in readiness. Then the four of them marched boldly into the castle.

Everywhere—in the courtyard, in the stables, and now in the various rooms of the castle—they saw great

numbers of richly clad men all of whom, masters and
servants alike, had been turned to stone.

They went on from one room to another until they
reached the banquet hall. This was brilliantly lighted
and the table, with food and drink in abundance, was
set for four persons. They waited, expecting some
one to appear, but no one came. At last, overpowered
by hunger, they sat down and ate and drank most
heartily.

After supper they began to look about for a place
to sleep. It was then without warning that the doors
burst open and the magician appeared. He was a bent
old man with a bald head and a gray beard that
reached to his knees. He was dressed in a long black
robe and he had, instead of a belt, three iron bands
about his waist.

He led in a beautiful lady dressed in white with
a silver girdle and a crown of pearls. Her face was
deathly pale and as sad as the grave. The prince
recognized her instantly and sprang forward to meet
her. Before he could speak, the magician raised his
hand and said:

" I know why you have come. It is to carry off
this princess. Very well, take her. If you can guard
her for three nights so that she won't escape you, she

is yours. But if she escapes you, then you and your men will suffer the fate of all those who have come before you and be turned into stone."

Then when he had motioned the princess to a seat, he turned and left the hall.

The prince could not take his eyes from the princess, she was so beautiful. He tried to talk to her, asking her many questions, but she made him no answer. She might have been marble the way she never smiled and never looked at any of them.

He seated himself beside her, determined to stay all night on guard in order to prevent her escape. For greater security Longshanks stretched himself out on the floor like a strap and wound himself around the room the whole length of the wall. Girth sat in the doorway and puffed himself out until he filled that space so completely that not even a mouse could slip through. Keen took his place by a pillar in the middle of the hall.

But, alas, in a few moments they all grew heavy with drowsiness and in the end slept soundly all night long.

In the morning in the early dawn the prince awoke and with a pain in his heart that was like a blow from a dagger, he saw that the princess was gone. Instantly he aroused his men and asked them what was to be done.

" It's all right, master, don't worry," said Keen as he took a long look through the window. " I see her now. A hundred miles from here is a forest, in the midst of the forest an ancient oak, on the top of the oak an acorn. The princess is that acorn. Let Long-shanks take me on his shoulders and we'll go get her."

Longshanks picked Keen up, stretched himself out, and set forth. He took ten miles at a stride and in the time it would take you or me to run around a cottage, here he was back again with the acorn in his hand. He gave it to the prince.

"Drop it, master, on the floor."

The prince dropped the acorn and instantly the princess appeared.

As the sun came over the mountain tops the doors slammed open and the magician entered. A crafty smile was on his face. But when he saw the princess the smile changed to a scowl, he growled in rage, and bang! one of the iron bands about his waist burst asunder. Then he took the princess by the hand and dragged her off.

That whole day the prince had nothing to do but wander about the castle and look at all the strange and curious things it contained. It seemed as if at some one instant all life had been arrested. In one hall he saw a prince who had been turned into stone while he was brandishing his sword. The sword was still uplifted. In another room there was a stone knight who was taken in the act of flight. He had stumbled on the threshold but he had not yet fallen. A serving man sat under the chimney eating his supper. With one hand he was reaching a piece of roast meat to his mouth. Days, months, perhaps years had gone by, but the meat had not yet touched his lips. There were many others, all of them still in whatever position they happened to be when the magician had cried: " Be ye turned into stone! "

In the courtyard and the stables the prince found many fine horses overtaken by the same fate.

Outside the castle everything was equally dead and silent. There were trees but they had no leaves, there was a river but it didn't flow, and no fish could live in its waters. There wasn't a singing bird anywhere, and there wasn't even one tiny flower.

In the morning, at noon, and at supper-time the prince and his companions found a rich feast prepared for them. Unseen hands served them food and poured them wine.

Then after supper, as on the preceding night, the doors burst open and the magician led in the princess, whom he handed over to the prince to guard for the second night.

Of course the prince and his men determined to fight off drowsiness this time with all their strength. But in spite of this determination again they fell asleep. At dawn the prince awoke and saw that the princess was gone.

He jumped up and shook Keen by the shoulder.

"Wake up, Keen, wake up! Where is the princess?"

Keen rubbed his eyes, took one look out of the window, and said:

"There, I see her. Two hundred miles from here is a mountain, in the mountain is a rock, in the rock a precious stone. That stone is the princess. If Longshanks will carry me over there we'll get her."

Longshanks put Keen on his shoulder, stretched himself out until he was able to go twenty miles at a stride, and off he went. Keen fixed his glowing eyes on the mountain and the mountain crumbled. Then the rock that was inside the mountain broke into a thousand pieces and there was the precious stone glittering among the pieces.

They picked it up and carried it back to the prince. As soon as he dropped it on the floor the princess re-appeared.

When the magician came in and found her there, his eyes sparkled with anger, and bang! the second of his iron bands cracked and burst asunder. Rumbling and growling he led the princess away.

That day passed as the day before. After supper the magician brought back the princess and, looking fiercely at the prince, he sneered and said: "Now we'll see who wins, you or I."

This night the prince and his men tried harder than ever to stay awake. They didn't even allow themselves to sit down but kept walking. All in vain. One after another they fell asleep on their feet and again the princess escaped.

In the morning the prince, as usual, was the first to awake. When he saw the princess was gone, he aroused Keen.

"Wake up, Keen!" he cried. "Look out and tell me where the princess is."

This time Keen had to look long before he saw her.

"Master, she is far away. Three hundred miles from here there is a black sea. At the bottom of that sea is a shell. In that shell is a golden ring. That ring is the princess. But don't be worried, master, we'll get her. This time let Longshanks take Girth as well as me, for we may need him."

So Longshanks put Keen on one shoulder and Girth on the other. Then he stretched himself out until he was able to cover thirty miles at a stride. When they reached the black sea Keen showed Longshanks where to reach down in the water for the shell. Longshanks reached down as far as he could but not far enough to touch bottom.

"Wait, comrades, wait a bit," said Girth. "Now it's my turn to help."

With that he puffed himself out and out as far as he could. Then he lay down on the beach and began drinking up the sea. He drank it in such great gulps that soon Longshanks was able to reach bottom and to get the shell. Longshanks took out the ring and then, putting his comrades on his shoulders, started back for the castle. He was not able to go fast, for Girth, with half the sea in his stomach, was very heavy. At last in desperation Longshanks turned Girth upside down and shook him and instantly the great plain upon which he emptied him turned into a huge lake. It was all poor Girth could do to scramble out of the water and back to Longshanks' shoulder.

Meanwhile at the castle the prince was awaiting his men in great anxiety. Morning was breaking and still they did not come. As the first rays of the sun shot over the mountain tops the doors slammed open and the magician stood on the threshold. He glanced around and when he saw that the princess was not there he gave a mocking laugh and entered.

But at that very instant there was the crash of a breaking window, a golden ring struck the floor, and lo! the princess! Keen had seen in time the danger that was threatening the prince and Longshanks had hurled the ring through the window.

The magician bellowed with rage until the castle shook and then, bang! the third iron band burst asunder and from what had once been the magician a black crow arose and flew out of the broken window and was never seen again.

Instantly the beautiful princess blushed like a rose and was able to speak and to thank the prince for delivering her.

Everything in the castle came to life. The prince with the uplifted sword finished his stroke and put the sword into its scabbard. The knight who was stumbling fell and jumped up holding his nose to see whether he still had it. The serving man under the chimney put the meat into his mouth and kept on eating. And so every one finished what he had been doing at the moment of enchantment. The horses, too, came to life and stamped and neighed.

Around the castle the trees burst into leaf. Flowers covered the meadows. High in the heavens the lark sang, and in the flowing river there were shoals of tiny fish. Everything was alive again, everything happy.

The knights who had been restored to life gathered in the hall to thank the prince for their deliverance. But the prince said to them:

" You have nothing to thank me for. If it had not been for these, my three trusty servants, Longshanks, Girth, and Keen, I should have met the same fate as you."

The prince set out at once on his journey home with his bride and his three serving men. When he reached home the old king, who had given him up for lost, wept for joy at his unexpected return.

All the knights whom the prince had rescued were invited to the wedding which took place at once and lasted for three weeks.

When it was over, Longshanks, Girth, and Keen presented themselves to the young king and told him that they were again going out into the world to look for work. The young king urged them to stay.

" I will give you everything you need as long as you live," he promised them, " and you won't have to exert yourselves at all."

But such an idle life was not to their liking. So they took their leave and started out again and to this day they are still knocking around somewhere.

THE THREE GOLDEN HAIRS

THE STORY OF A CHARCOAL-BURNER'S SON
WHO MARRIED A PRINCESS

THE THREE GOLDEN HAIRS

THERE was once a king who took great delight in hunting. One day he followed a stag a great distance into the forest. He went on and on until he lost his way. Night fell and the king by happy chance came upon a clearing where a charcoal-burner had a cottage. The king asked the charcoal-burner to lead him out of the forest and offered to pay him handsomely.

" I'd be glad to go with you," the charcoal-burner said, " but my wife is expecting the birth of a child and I cannot leave her. It is too late for you to start out alone. Won't you spend the night here? Lie down on some hay in the garret and tomorrow I'll be your guide."

The king had to accept this arrangement. He climbed into the garret and lay down on the floor. Soon afterwards a son was born to the charcoal-burner.

At midnight the king noticed a strange light in the room below him. He peeped through a chink in the boards and saw the charcoal-burner asleep, his wife lying in a dead faint, and three old women, all in white, standing over the baby, each holding a lighted taper in her hand.

The first old woman said: "My gift to this boy is that he shall encounter great dangers."

The second said: "My gift to him is that he shall go safely through them all, and live long."

The third one said: "And I give him for wife the baby daughter born this night to the king who lies upstairs on the straw."

The three old women blew out their tapers and all was quiet. They were the Fates.

The king felt as though a sword had been thrust into his heart. He lay awake till morning trying to think out some plan by which he could thwart the will of the three old Fates.

When day broke the child began to cry and the charcoal-burner woke up. Then he saw that his wife had died during the night.

"Ah, my poor motherless child," he cried, "what shall I do with you now?"

"Give me the baby," the king said. "I'll see that he's looked after properly and I'll give you enough money to keep you the rest of your life."

The charcoal-burner was delighted with this offer and the king went away promising to send at once for the baby.

A few days later when he reached his palace he was met with the joyful news that a beautiful little baby daughter had been born to him. He asked the time of her birth, and of course it was on the very night when he saw the Fates. Instead of being pleased at the safe arrival of the baby princess, the king frowned.

Then he called one of his stewards and said to him: " Go into the forest in a direction that I shall tell you. You will find there a cottage where a charcoal-burner lives. Give him this money and get from him a little child. Take the child and on your way back drown it. Do as I say or I shall have you drowned."

The steward went, found the charcoal-burner, and took the child. He put it into a basket and carried it away. As he was crossing a broad river he dropped the basket into the water.

" Goodnight to you, little son-in-law that nobody wanted! " the king said when he heard what the steward had done.

He supposed of course that the baby was drowned. But it wasn't. Its little basket floated in the water like a cradle, and the baby slept as if the river were singing it a lullaby. It floated down with the current past a fisherman's cottage. The fisherman saw it, got into his boat, and went after it. When he found what the basket contained he was overjoyed. At once he carried the baby to his wife and said:

" You have always wanted a little son and here you have one. The river has given him to us."

The fisherman's wife was delighted and brought up the child as her own. They named him Plavachek, which means a little boy who has come floating on the water.

The river flowed on and the days went by and Plavachek grew from a baby to a boy and then into a handsome youth, the handsomest by far in the whole countryside.

One day the king happened to ride that way unattended. It was hot and he was thirsty. He beckoned to the fisherman to get him a drink of fresh water. Plavachek brought it to him. The king looked at the handsome youth in astonishment.

" You have a fine lad," he said to the fisherman. " Is he your own son? "

" He is, yet he isn't," the fisherman answered. " Just twenty years ago a little baby in a basket floated down the river. We took him in and he has been ours ever since."

A mist rose before the king's eyes and he went deathly pale, for he knew at once that Plavachek was the child that he had ordered drowned.

Soon he recovered himself and jumping from his horse he said: " I need a messenger to send to my palace and I have no one with me. Could this youth go for me? "

" Your majesty has but to command," the fisherman said, " and Plavachek will go."

The king sat down and wrote a letter to the queen. This is what he said:

" Have the young man who delivers this letter run through with a sword at once. He is a dangerous enemy. Let him be dispatched before I return. Such is my will."

He folded the letter, made it secure, and sealed it with his own signet.

Plavachek took the letter and started out with it at once. He had to go through a deep forest where he missed the path and lost his way. He struggled on through underbrush and thicket until it began to grow dark. Then he met an old woman who said to him:

" Where are you going, Plavachek? "

" I'm carrying this letter to the king's palace and I've lost my way. Can you put me on the right road, mother? "

" You can't get there today," the old woman said. " It's dark now. Spend the night with me. You won't be with a stranger, for I'm your old godmother."

Plavachek allowed himself to be persuaded and presently he saw before him a pretty little house that seemed at that moment to have sprung out of the ground.

During the night while Plavachek was asleep, the old woman took the letter out of his pocket and put in another that read as follows:

" Have the young man who delivers this letter married to our daughter at once. He is my destined son-in-law. Let the wedding take place before I return. Such is my will."

The next day Plavachek delivered the letter and as soon as the queen read it, she gave orders at once for the wedding. Both she and her daughter were much taken with the handsome youth and gazed at him with tender eyes. As for Plavachek he fell instantly in love with the princess and was delighted to marry her.

Some days after the wedding the king returned

and when he heard what had happened he flew into a violent rage at the queen.

" But," protested the queen, " you yourself ordered me to have him married to our daughter before you came back. Here is your letter."

The king took the letter and examined it carefully. The handwriting, the seal, the paper—all were his own.

He called his son-in-law and questioned him.

Plavachek related how he had lost his way in the forest and spent the night with his godmother.

" What does your godmother look like? " the king asked.

Plavachek described her.

From the description the king recognized her as the same old woman who had promised the princess to the charcoal-burner's son twenty years before.

He looked at Plavachek thoughtfully and at last he said:

" What's done can't be undone. However, young man, you can't expect to be my son-in-law for nothing. If you want my daughter you must bring me for dowry three of the golden hairs of old Grandfather Knowitall."

He thought to himself that this would be an impossible task and so would be a good way to get rid of an undesirable son-in-law.

Plavachek took leave of his bride and started off. He didn't know which way to go. Who would know? Everybody talked about old Grandfather Knowitall, but nobody seemed to know where to find him. Yet Plavachek had a Fate for a godmother, so it wasn't likely that he would miss the right road.

He traveled long and far, going over wooded hills and desert plains and crossing deep rivers. He came at last to a black sea.

There he saw a boat and an old ferryman.

" God bless you, old ferryman! " he said.

" May God grant that prayer, young traveler! Where are you going? "

" I'm going to old Grandfather Knowitall to get three of his golden hairs."

" Oho! I have long been hunting for just such a messenger as you! For twenty years I have been ferrying people across this black sea and nobody has come to relieve me. If you promise to ask Grandfather Knowitall when my work will end, I'll ferry you over."

Plavachek promised and the boatman took him across.

Plavachek traveled on until he came to a great city that was in a state of decay. Before the city he met an old man who had a staff in his hand, but even with the staff he could scarcely crawl along.

"God bless you, old grandfather!" Plavachek said.

"May God grant that prayer, handsome youth! Where are you going?"

"I am going to old Grandfather Knowitall to get three of his golden hairs."

"Indeed! We have been waiting a long time for just such a messenger as you! I must lead you at once to the king."

So he took him to the king and the king said: "Ah, so you are going on an errand to Grandfather Knowitall! We have an apple-tree here that used to bear apples of youth. If any one ate one of those apples, no matter how aged he was, he'd become young again. But, alas, for twenty years now our tree has borne no fruit. If you promise to ask Grandfather Knowitall if there is any help for us, I will reward you handsomely."

Plavachek gave the king his promise and the king bid him godspeed.

Plavachek traveled on until he reached another great

city that was half in ruins. Not far from the city a man was burying his father, and tears as big as peas were rolling down his cheek.

"God bless you, mournful grave-digger!" Plavachek said.

"May God grant that prayer, kind traveler! Where are you going?"

"I'm going to old Grandfather Knowitall to get three of his golden hairs."

"To Grandfather Knowitall! What a pity you didn't come sooner! Our king has long been waiting for just such a messenger as you! I must lead you to him."

So he took Plavachek to the king and the king said to him: "So you're going on an errand to Grandfather Knowitall. We have a well here that used to flow with the water of life. If any one drank of it, no matter how sick he was, he would get well. Nay, if he were already dead, this water, sprinkled upon him, would bring him back to life. But, alas, for twenty years now the well has gone dry. If you promise to ask Grandfather Knowitall if there is help for us, I will reward you handsomely."

Plavachek gave the king his promise and the king bid him godspeed.

After that Plavachek traveled long and far into a black forest. Deep in the forest he came upon a broad green meadow full of beautiful flowers and in its midst a golden palace glittering as though it were on fire. This was the palace of Grandfather Knowitall.

Plavachek entered and found nobody there but an old woman who sat spinning in a corner.

" Welcome, Plavachek," she said. " I am delighted to see you again."

He looked at the old woman and saw that she was his godmother with whom he had spent the night when he was carrying the letter to the palace.

" What has brought you here, Plavachek?" she asked.

" The king, godmother. He says I can't be his son-in-law for nothing. I have to give a dowry. So he has sent me to old Grandfather Knowitall to get three of his golden hairs."

The old woman smiled and said: " Do you know who Grandfather Knowitall is? Why, he's the bright Sun who goes everywhere and sees everything. I am his mother. In the morning he's a little lad, at noon he's a grown man, and in the evening an old grandfather. I will get you three of the golden hairs from his golden head, for I must not be a godmother for nothing! But, my lad, you mustn't remain where you are. My son is kind, but if he comes home hungry he might want to roast you and eat you for his supper. There's an empty tub over there and I'll just cover you with it."

Plavachek begged his godmother to get from Grandfather Knowitall the answers for the three questions he had promised to ask.

"I will," said the old woman, "and do you listen carefully to what he says."

Suddenly there was the rushing sound of a mighty wind outside and the Sun, an old grandfather with a golden head, flew in by the western window. He sniffed the air suspiciously.

"Phew! Phew!" he cried. "I smell human flesh! Have you any one here, mother?"

"Star of the day, whom could I have here without your seeing him? The truth is you've been flying all day long over God's world and your nose is filled with the smell of human flesh. That's why you still smell it when you come home in the evening."

The old man said nothing more and sat down to his supper.

After supper he laid his head on the old woman's lap and fell sound asleep. The old woman pulled out a golden hair and threw it on the floor. It twanged like the string of a violin.

"What is it, mother?" the old man said. "What is it?"

"Nothing, my boy, nothing. I was asleep and had a wonderful dream."

"What did you dream about, mother?"

"I dreamt about a city where they had a well of living water. If any one drank of it, no matter how sick he was, he would get well. Nay, if he were already dead, this water, sprinkled on him, would bring him back to life. For the last twenty years the well has gone dry. Is there anything to be done to make it flow again?"

"Yes. There's a frog sitting on the spring that feeds the well. Let them kill the frog and clean out the well and the water will flow as before."

When he fell asleep again the old woman pulled out another golden hair and threw it on the floor.

"What is it, mother?"

"Nothing, my boy, nothing. I was asleep again and I had a wonderful dream. I dreamt of a city where they had an apple-tree that bore apples of youth. If any one ate one of those apples, no matter how aged he was, he'd become young again. But for twenty years the tree has borne no fruit. Can anything be done about it?"

"Yes. In the roots of the tree there is a snake that takes its strength. Let them kill the snake and transplant the tree. Then it will bear fruit as before."

He fell asleep again and the old woman pulled out a third golden hair.

"Why won't you let me sleep, mother?" he complained, and started to sit up.

"Lie still, my boy, lie still. I didn't intend to wake you, but a heavy sleep fell upon me and I had another wonderful dream. I dreamt of a boatman on the black sea. For twenty years he has been ferrying that boat and no one has offered to relieve him. When will he be relieved?"

"Ah, but that boatman is the son of a stupid mother! Why doesn't he thrust the oar into the hand of some one else and jump ashore himself? Then the other man would have to be ferryman in his place. But now let me be quiet. I must get up early tomorrow morning and go and dry the tears which the king's daughter sheds every night for her husband, the charcoal-burner's son, whom the king has sent to get three of my golden hairs."

In the morning there was again the rushing sound

of a mighty wind outside and a beautiful golden child
—no longer an old man—awoke on his mother's lap.
It was the glorious Sun. He bade his mother farewell and flew out by an eastern window.

The old woman turned over the tub and said to
Plavachek: "Here are the three golden hairs for you.
You also have Grandfather Knowitall's answers to
your three questions. Now good-by. As you will
need me no more, you will never see me again."

Plavachek thanked his godmother most gratefully
and departed.

When he reached the first city the king asked him
what news he brought.

"Good news!" Plavachek said. "Have the well
cleaned out and kill the frog that sits on its spring.
If you do this the water will flow again as it used to."

The king ordered this to be done at once and when
he saw the water beginning to bubble up and flow
again, he made Plavachek a present of twelve horses,
white as swans, laden with as much gold and silver
as they could carry.

When Plavachek came to the second city and the
king of that city asked him what news he brought,
he said:

"Good news! Have the apple tree dug up. At

its roots you will find a snake. Kill the snake and replant the tree. Then it will bear fruit as it used to."

The king had this done at once and during the night the tree burst into bloom and bore great quantities of fruit. The king was delighted and made Plavachek a present of twelve horses, black as ravens, laden with as much riches as they could carry.

Plavachek traveled on and when he came to the black sea, the boatman asked him had he the answer to his question.

"Yes, I have," said Plavachek, "but you must ferry me over before I tell you."

The boatman wanted to hear the answer at once, but Plavachek was firm. So the old man ferried him across with his twelve white horses and his twelve black horses.

When Plavachek was safely landed, he said: "The next person who comes to be ferried over, thrust the oar into his hand and do you jump ashore. Then the other man will have to be boatman in your place."

Plavachek traveled home to the palace. The king could scarcely believe his eyes when he saw the three golden hairs of Grandfather Knowitall. The princess wept again, not for sorrow this time but for joy at her bridegroom's return.

"But, Plavachek," the king gasped, "where did you get these beautiful horses and all these riches?"

"I earned them," said Plavachek proudly. Then he related how he helped one king who had a tree of the apples of youth and another king who had a well of the water of life.

"Apples of youth! Water of life!" the king kept repeating softly to himself. "If I ate one of those apples I should become young again! If I were dead the water of life would restore me!"

He lost no time in starting out in quest of the apples of youth and the water of life. And do you know, he hasn't come back yet!

So Plavachek, the charcoal-burner's son, became the king's son-in-law as the old Fate foretold.

As for the king, well, I fear he's still ferrying that boat across the black sea!

THE FLAMING HORSE

THE STORY OF A COUNTRY WHERE THE SUN NEVER SHINES

THE FLAMING HORSE

THERE was once a land that was dreary and dark as the grave, for the sun of heaven never shone upon it. The king of the country had a wonderful horse that had, growing right on his forehead, a flaming sun. In order that his subjects might have the light that is necessary for life, the king had this horse led back and forth from one end of his dark kingdom to the other. Wherever he went his flaming head shone out and it seemed like beautiful day.

Suddenly this wonderful horse disappeared. Heavy darkness that nothing could dispel settled down on the country. Fear spread among the people and soon they were suffering terrible poverty, for they were unable to cultivate the fields or do anything else that would earn them a livelihood. Confusion increased until the king saw that the whole country was likely to perish. In order then, if possible, to save his people, he gathered his army together and set out in search of the missing horse.

Through heavy darkness they groped their way slowly and with difficulty to the far boundaries of the kingdom. At last they reached the ancient forests that bordered the neighboring state and they saw gleaming through the trees faint rays of the sunshine with which that kingdom was blessed.

Here they came upon a small lonely cottage which the king entered in order to find out where he was and to ask directions for moving forward.

A man was sitting at the table reading diligently from a large open book. When the king bowed to him, he raised his eyes, returned the greeting, and stood up. His whole appearance showed that he was no ordinary man but a seer.

" I was just reading about you," he said to the king, " that you were gone in search of the flaming horse. Exert yourself no further, for you will never find him. But trust the enterprise to me and I will get him for you."

" If you do that, my man," the king said, " I will pay you royally."

" I seek no reward. Return home at once with your army, for your people need you. Only leave here with me one of your serving men."

The king did exactly as the seer advised and went home at once.

The next day the seer and his man set forth. They journeyed far and long until they had crossed six different countries. Then they went on into the seventh country which was ruled over by three brothers who had married three sisters, the daughters of a witch.

They made their way to the front of the royal palace, where the seer said to his man: " Do you stay here while I go in and find out whether the kings are at home. It is they who stole the flaming horse and the youngest brother rides him."

Then the seer transformed himself into a green bird and flew up to the window of the eldest queen and flitted about and pecked until she opened the window and let him into her chamber. When she let him in, he alighted on her white hand and the queen was as happy as a child.

" You pretty thing! " she said, playing with him. " If my husband were home how pleased he would be! But he's off visiting a third of his kingdom and he won't be home until evening."

Suddenly the old witch came into the room and as soon as she saw the bird she shrieked to her daughter: " Wring the neck of that cursed bird, or it will stain you with blood! "

"Why should it stain me with blood, the dear innocent thing!"

"Dear innocent mischief!" shrieked the witch. "Here, give it to me and I'll wring its neck!"

She tried to catch the bird, but the bird changed itself into a man and was already out of the door before they knew what had become of him.

After that he changed himself again into a green bird and flew up to the window of the second sister. He pecked at it until she opened it and let him in. Then he flitted about her, settling first on one of her white hands, then on the other.

"What a dear bird you are!" cried the queen. "How you would please my husband if he were at home. But he's off visiting two-thirds of his kingdom and he won't be back until tomorrow evening."

At that moment the witch ran into the room and as soon as she saw the bird she shrieked out: "Wring the neck of that wretched bird, or it will stain you with blood!"

"Why should it stain me with blood?" the daughter answered. "The dear innocent thing!"

"Dear innocent mischief!" shrieked the witch. "Here, give it to me and I'll wring its neck!"

She reached out to catch the bird, but in less time

than it takes to clap a hand, the bird had changed itself into a man who ran through the door and was gone before they knew where he was.

A moment later he again changed himself into a green bird and flew up to the window of the youngest queen. He flitted about and pecked until she opened the window and let him in. Then he alighted at once on her white hand and this pleased her so much that she laughed like a child and played with him.

" Oh, what a dear bird you are! " she cried. " How you would delight my husband if he were home. But he's off visiting all three parts of his kingdom and he won't be back until the day after tomorrow in the evening."

At that moment the old witch rushed into the room. " Wring the neck of that cursed bird! " she shrieked, " or it will stain you with blood."

" My dear mother," the queen answered, " why should it stain me with blood—beautiful innocent creature that it is! "

" Beautiful innocent mischief! " shrieked the witch. " Here, give it to me and I'll wring its neck! "

But at that moment the bird changed itself into a man, disappeared through the door, and they never saw him again.

The seer knew now where the kings were and when they would come home. So he made his plans accordingly. He ordered his servant to follow him and they set out from the city at a quick pace. They went on until they came to a bridge which the three kings as they came back would have to cross.

The seer and his man hid themselves under the bridge and lay there in wait until evening. As the sun sank behind the mountains, they heard the clatter of hoofs approaching the bridge. It was the eldest king returning home. At the bridge his horse stumbled on a log which the seer had rolled there.

"What scoundrel has thrown a log here?" cried the king angrily.

Instantly the seer leaped out from under the bridge and demanded of the king how he dared to call him a scoundrel. Clamoring for satisfaction he drew his sword and attacked the king. The king, too, drew sword and defended himself, but after a short struggle 'he fell from his horse dead. The seer bound the dead king to his horse and then with a cut of the whip started the horse homewards.

The seer hid himself again and he and his man lay in wait until the next evening.

On that evening near sunset the second king came

riding up to the bridge. When he saw the ground sprinkled with blood, he cried out: " Surely there has been a murder here! Who has dared to commit such a crime in my kingdom!"

At these words the seer leaped out from under the bridge, drew his sword, and shouted: " How dare you insult me? Defend yourself as best you can!"

The king drew, but after a short struggle he, too, yielded up his life to the sword of the seer.

The seer bound the dead king to his horse and with a cut of the whip started the horse homewards.

Then the seer hid himself again under the bridge and he and his man lay there in wait until the third evening.

On the third evening just at sunset the youngest king came galloping home on the flaming steed. He was hurrying fast because he had been delayed. But when he saw red blood at the bridge he stopped short and looked around.

" What audacious villain," he cried, " has dared to kill a man in my kingdom!"

Hardly had he spoken when the seer stood before him with drawn sword demanding satisfaction for the insult of his words.

"I don't know how I've insulted you," the king said, "unless you're the murderer."

When the seer refused to parley, the king, too, drew his sword and defended himself.

To overcome the first two kings had been mere play for the seer, but it was no play this time. They both fought until their swords were broken and still victory was doubtful.

"We shall accomplish nothing with swords," the seer said. "That is plain. I tell you what: let us turn ourselves into wheels and start rolling down the hill and the wheel that gets broken let him yield."

"Good!" said the king. "I'll be a cartwheel and you be a lighter wheel."

"No, no," the seer answered quickly. "You be the light wheel and I'll be the cartwheel."

To this the king agreed. So they went up the hill, turned themselves into wheels and started rolling down. The cartwheel went whizzing into the lighter wheel and broke its spokes.

"There!" cried the seer, rising up from the cartwheel. "I am victor!"

"Not so, brother, not so!" said the king, standing before the seer. "You only broke my fingers! Now I tell you what: let us change ourselves into two flames and let the flame that burns up the other be victor. I'll be a red flame and do you be a white one."

" Oh, no," the seer interrupted. " You be the white flame and I'll be the red one."

The king agreed to this. So they went back to the road that led to the bridge, turned themselves into flames, and began burning each other mercilessly. But neither was able to burn up the other.

Suddenly a beggar came down the road, an old man with a long gray beard and a bald head, with a scrip at his side and a heavy staff in his hand.

" Father," the white flame said, " get some water and pour it on the red flame and I'll give you a penny."

But the red flame called out quickly: " Not so, father! Get some water and pour it on the white flame and I'll give you a shilling! "

Now of course the shilling appealed to the beggar more than the penny. So he got some water, poured it on the white flame and that was the end of the king.

The red flame turned into a man who seized the flaming horse by the bridle, mounted him and, after he had rewarded the beggar, called his servant and rode off.

Meanwhile at the royal palace there was deep sorrow for the murdered kings. The halls were draped in black and people came from miles around to gaze at the mutilated bodies of the two elder brothers which the horses had carried home.

The old witch was beside herself with rage. As soon as she had devised a plan whereby she could avenge the murder of her sons-in-law, she took her three daughters under her arm, mounted an iron rake, and sailed off through the air.

The seer and his man had already covered a good part of their journey and were hurrying on over rough mountains and across desert plains, when the servant was taken with a terrible hunger. There wasn't anything in sight that he could eat, not even a wild berry. Then suddenly they came upon an apple tree that was bending beneath a load of ripe fruit. The apples were red and pleasant to the sight and sent out a fragrance that was most inviting.

The servant was delighted. " Glory to God! " he cried. " Now I can feast to my heart's content on these apples! "

He was already running to the tree when the seer called him back.

" Wait! Don't touch them! I will pick them for you myself! "

But instead of picking an apple, the seer drew his

sword and struck a mighty blow into the apple tree. Red blood gushed forth.

"Just see, my man! You would have perished if you had eaten one apple. This apple tree is the eldest queen, whom her mother, the witch, placed here for our destruction."

Presently they came to a spring. Its water bubbled up clear as crystal and most tempting to the tired traveler.

"Ah," said the servant, "since we can get nothing better, at least we can take a drink of this good water."

"Wait!" cried the seer. "I will draw some for you."

But instead of drawing water he plunged his naked sword into the middle of the spring. Instantly it was covered with blood and blood began to spurt from the spring in thick streams.

"This is the second queen, whom her mother, the witch, placed here to work our doom."

Presently they came to a rosebush covered with beautiful red roses that scented all the air with their fragrance.

"What beautiful roses!" said the servant. "I have never seen any such in all my life. I'll go pluck a few. As I can't eat or drink, I'll comfort myself with roses."

" Don't dare to pluck them! " cried the seer. " I'll pluck them for you."

With that he cut into the bush with his sword and red blood spurted out as though he had cut a human vein.

" This is the youngest queen," said the seer, " whom her mother, the witch, placed here in the hope of revenging herself on us for the death of her sons-in-law."

After that they proceeded without further adventures.

When they crossed the boundaries of the dark kingdom, the sun in the horse's forehead sent out its blessed rays in all directions. Everything came to life. The earth rejoiced and covered itself with flowers.

The king felt he could never thank the seer enough and he offered him the half of his kingdom.

But the seer replied: " You are the king. Keep on ruling over the whole of your kingdom and let me return to my cottage in peace."

He bade the king farewell and departed.

THE THREE CITRONS

THE STORY OF A PRINCE
WHO CLIMBED THE GLASS HILL

THE THREE CITRONS

ONCE upon a time there was an aged king who had an only son. One day he called the prince to him and said: "My son, you see that my head is white. Soon I shall be closing my eyes and you are not yet settled in life. Marry, my son, marry at once so that I can bless you before I die."

The prince made no answer but he took the king's words to heart and pondered them. He would gladly have done as his father wished but there was no young girl upon whom his affections were set.

One day when he was sitting in the garden, wondering what to do, an old woman suddenly appeared before him.

"Go," she said, "to the top of the Glass Hill, pluck the Three Citrons, and you will get a wife in whom your heart will delight." With that she disappeared as mysteriously as she had come.

Her words went through the prince's soul like a bright dart. Instantly he determined, come what might, to find the Glass Hill and to pluck the Three Citrons. He told his father his intention and the old king fitted him out for the journey and gave him his blessing.

For a long time the prince wandered over wooded mountains and desert plains without seeing or even hearing anything of the Glass Hill and the Three Citrons. One day, worn out with his long journey, he threw himself down in the shade of a wide-spreading linden tree. As his father's sword, which he wore at his side, clanked on the ground, twelve ravens began cawing from the top of the tree. Frightened by the clanking of the sword, they raised their wings and flew off.

The prince jumped to his feet. " Those are the first living creatures I have seen for many a day. I'll go in the direction they have taken," he said to himself, " and perhaps I'll have better luck."

So he traveled on and after three days and three nights a high castle came in view.

" Thank God! " he exclaimed, pushing joyfully ahead. " I shall soon have human companionship once more."

The castle was built entirely of lead. The twelve ravens circled above it and in front of it stood an old woman leaning on a long leaden staff. She was a Yezibaba. Now you must know that a Yezibaba is an ugly old witch with a hooked nose, a bristly face, and long scrawny hands. She's a bad old thing usually, but sometimes, if you take her fancy, she's kind.

This time when she looked the prince over she shook her head at him in a friendly way.

"Yi, yi, my boy, how did you get here? Why, not even a little bird or a tiny butterfly comes here, much less a human being! You'd better escape if life is dear to you, or my son, when he comes home, will eat you!"

"No, no, old mother, don't make me go," begged the prince. "I have come to you for advice to know whether you can tell me anything about the Glass Hill and the Three Citrons."

"No, I have never heard a word about the Glass Hill," Yezibaba said. "But wait until my son comes. He may be able to tell you something. Yes, yes, I'll manage to save you somehow. Go hide under the besom and stay there until I call you."

The mountains rumbled and the castle trembled and Yezibaba whispered to the prince that her son was coming.

"Phew! Phew! I smell human meat! I'll eat it!" shouted Yezibaba's son while he was still in the doorway. He struck the ground with his leaden club and the whole castle shook.

" No, no, my son, don't talk that way. It's true there is a pretty youth here, but he's come to ask you about something."

" Well, if he wants to ask me something, let him come out and ask."

" Yes, my son, he will, but only when you promise me that you will do nothing to him."

" Well, I won't do anything to him. Now let him come out."

The prince hidden under the besom was shaking like an aspen leaf, for when he peeped through the twigs he saw an ogre so huge that he himself would reach up only to his knees. Happily the ogre had guaranteed his life before Yezibaba ordered him out.

" Well, well, well, you little June bug!" shouted the ogre. " What are you afraid of? Where have you been? What do you want?"

" What do I want?" repeated the prince. " I have been wandering in these mountains a long time and I can't find what I'm seeking. So I've come to you to ask whether you can tell me something about the Glass Hill and the Three Citrons."

Yezibaba's son wrinkled his forehead. He thought

for a moment and then, lowering his voice a little, he said: " I've never heard of any Glass Hill around here. But I tell you what you do: go on to my brother in arms who lives in the Silver Castle and ask him. Maybe he'll be able to tell you. But I can't let you go away hungry. That would never do! Hi, mother, bring out the dumplings! "

Old Yezibaba placed a large dish on the table and her giant son sat down.

"Well, come on! Eat! " he shouted to the prince.

When the prince took the first dumpling and bit into it, he almost broke two of his teeth, for the dumpling was made of lead.

"Well," shouted Yezibaba's son, "why don't you eat? Doesn't the dumpling taste good? "

" Oh, yes, very good," said the prince, politely, " but just now I'm not hungry."

"Well, if you're not hungry now you will be later. Put a few in your pocket and eat them on your journey."

So, whether he wanted them or not, the prince had to put some leaden dumplings into his pocket. Then he took his leave of Yezibaba and her son and traveled on.

He went on and on for three days and three nights.

The farther he went, the more inhospitable became the country. Before him stretched a waste of mountains, behind him a waste of mountains with no living creature in sight.

Wearied with his long journey, he threw himself on the ground. His silver sword clanked sharply and at its sound twenty-four ravens circled above him, cawed in fright, and flew away.

"A good sign!" cried the prince. "I'll follow the ravens again!"

So on he went as fast as his legs could carry him until he came in sight of a tall castle. It was still far away, but even at that distance it shone and flashed, for it was built of pure silver.

In front of the castle stood an old woman, bent with age, and leaning on a long silver staff. This was the second Yezibaba.

"Yi, yi, my boy!" she cried. "How did you get here? Why, not even a little bird or a tiny butterfly comes here, much less a human being. You'd better escape if life is dear to you, or my son, when he comes home, will eat you!"

"No, no, old mother, he won't eat me. I bring greetings from his brother of the Leaden Castle."

"Well, if you bring greetings from the Leaden

Castle you are safe enough. Come in, my boy, and tell me your business."

" My business? For a long time, old mother, I've been looking for the Glass Hill and the Three Citrons, but I can't find them. So I've come to ask you whether you could tell me something about them."

" No, my boy, I don't know anything about the Glass Hill. But wait until my son comes. Perhaps he can help you. In the meantime hide yourself under the bed and don't come out until I call you."

The mountains rumbled and the castle trembled and the prince knew that Yezibaba's son was coming home.

" Phew! Phew! I smell human meat! I'll eat it! " bellowed the mighty fellow. He stood in the doorway and banged the ground with his silver club until the whole castle shook.

" No, no, my son," said Yezibaba, " don't talk that way! A pretty little chap has come bringing you greetings from your brother of the Leaden Castle."

" Well, if he's been at the Leaden Castle and came to no harm, he'll have nothing to fear from me either. Where is he? "

The prince slipped out from under the bed and stood before the ogre. Looking up at him was like looking at the top of the tallest pine tree.

" Well, little June bug, so you've been at my brother's, eh? "

" Yes," said the prince. " See, I still have the dumplings he gave me for the journey."

" I believe you. Well, what do you want? "

" What do I want? I came to ask you whether you could tell me something about the Glass Hill and the Three Citrons."

" H'm, it seems to me I used to hear something about them, but I forget. I tell you what you do: go to my brother of the Golden Castle and ask him. But wait! I can't let you go away hungry. Hi, mother, bring out the dumplings! "

Yezibaba brought the dumplings on a large silver dish and put them on the table.

" Eat! " shouted her son.

The prince saw they were silver dumplings, so he said he wasn't hungry just then, but he'd like to take some with him for the journey.

" Take as many as you want," shouted the ogre. " And give my greetings to my brother and my aunt."

So the prince took some silver dumplings, made suitable thanks, and departed.

He journeyed on from the Silver Castle three days and three nights, through dense forests and over rough mountains, not knowing where he was nor which way to turn. At last all worn out he threw himself down in the shade of a beech tree to rest. As the sword clanked on the ground, its silver voice rang out and a flock of thirty-six ravens circled over his head.

"Caw! Caw!" they croaked. Then, frightened by the sound of the sword, they flew away.

"Praise God!" cried the prince. "The Golden Castle can't be far!"

He jumped up and started eagerly off in the direction the ravens had taken. As he left a valley and climbed a little hill he saw before him a beautiful wide meadow in the midst of which stood the Golden Castle shining like the sun. Before the gate of the castle stood a bent old Yezibaba leaning on a golden staff.

"Yi, yi, my boy," she cried to the prince, "how did you get here? Why, not even a little bird or a tiny butterfly comes here, much less a human being! You'd better escape if life is dear to you, or my son, when he comes home, will eat you!"

"No, no, old mother, he won't eat me, for I bring him greetings from his brother of the Silver Castle!"

"Well, if you bring greetings from the Silver 'Castle you are safe enough. Come in, my boy, and tell me your business."

" My business, old mother? For a long time I've been wandering over these wild mountains in search of the Glass Hill and the Three Citrons. At the Silver Castle they sent me to you because they thought you might know something about them."

" The Glass Hill? No, I don't know where it is. But wait until my son comes. He will advise you where to go and what to do. Hide under the table and stay there till I call you."

The mountains rumbled and the castle trembled and Yezibaba's son came home.

" Phew! Phew! I smell human meat! I'll eat it! " he roared. He stood in the doorway and pounded the ground with his golden club until the whole castle shook.

" No, no, my son," said Yezibaba, " don't talk that way! A pretty little fellow has come bringing you greetings from your brother of the Silver Castle. If you won't harm him, I'll call him out."

" Well, if my brother didn't do anything to him, I won't either."

So the prince crawled out from under the table and stood before the giant. It was like standing beneath a high tower. He showed the ogre the silver dumplings as proof that he had been at the Silver Castle.

" Well, well, well, my little June bug," shouted the monstrous fellow, " tell me what it is you want! I'll advise you if I can! Don't be afraid! "

So the prince told him the purpose of his journey and asked him how to get to the Glass Hill and pluck the Three Citrons.

" Do you see that blackish lump over yonder? " the ogre said, pointing with his golden club. " That is the Glass Hill. On that hill stands a tree. From that tree hang the Three Citrons which send out fragrance for seven miles around. You will climb the Glass Hill, kneel beneath the tree, and reach up your hands. If the citrons are destined for you they will fall into your hands of their own accord. If they are not destined for you, you will not be able to pluck them no matter what you do. As you return, if you are hungry or thirsty, cut open one of the citrons and you will have food and drink in plenty. Go now with God's blessing. But wait! I can't let you go away hungry! Hi, mother, bring out the dumplings! "

Yezibaba set a large golden dish on the table.

" Eat! " her son shouted. " Or, if you are not hungry just now, put some in your pocket and eat them on the way."

The prince said that he was not hungry but that

he would be glad to take some of the golden dumplings with him and eat them later. Then he thanked the ogre most courteously for his hospitality and advice and took his leave.

He trudged quickly on from hill to dale, from dale to hill again, and never stopped until he reached the Glass Hill itself. Then he stood still as if turned into stone. The hill was high and steep and smooth with not so much as a scratch on its surface. Over its top spread out the branches of the magic tree upon which hung the Three Citrons. Their fragrance was so powerful that the prince almost fainted.

"Let it be as God wills!" he thought to himself. "But however the adventure is to come out, now that I'm here I must at least make the attempt."

So he began to claw his way up the smooth glass, but he hadn't gone many yards before his foot slipped and down he went so hard that he didn't know where he was or what had happened to him until he found himself sitting on the ground.

In his vexation he began to throw away the dumplings, thinking that perhaps their weight had dragged him down. He took one and threw it straight at the hill. Imagine his surprise to see it fix itself firmly in the glass. He threw a second and a third and there he had three steps on which he was able to stand with safety!

The prince was overjoyed. He threw dumpling after dumpling and each one of them became a step. First he threw the leaden ones, then the silver ones, and last of all the golden ones. On the steps made in this way he climbed higher and higher until he had reached the very summit of the hill. Then he knelt under the magic tree, lifted up his hands, and into them the Three Citrons dropped of their own accord!

Instantly the tree disappeared, the Glass Hill sank until it was lost, and when the prince came to himself there was neither tree nor hill to be seen, but only a wide plain.

Delighted with the outcome of his adventure, the prince turned homewards. At first he was too happy even to eat or drink. By the third day his stomach began to protest and he discovered that he was so hungry that he would have fallen ravenously upon a leaden dumpling if he had had one in his pocket. But his pocket, alas, was empty, and the country all about was as bare as the palm of his hand.

Then he remembered what the ogre of the Golden Castle had told him and he took out one of the Three Citrons. He cut it open, and what do you suppose happened? Out jumped a beautiful maiden fresh from the hand of God, who bowed low before him and exclaimed:

"Have you food ready for me? Have you drink ready for me? Have you pretty clothes ready for me?"

"Alas, beautiful creature," the prince sighed, "I have not. I have nothing for you to eat or to drink or to put on."

The lovely maiden clapped her hands three times, bowed before him, and disappeared.

"Ah," said the prince, "now I know what kind of citrons you are! I'll think twice before opening one of you again!"

Of the one he had opened he ate and drank his fill, and so refreshed, went on. He traveled three days and three nights and by that time he began to feel three times hungrier than before.

"God help me!" thought he. "I must eat something! There are still two citrons and if I cut open one there would still be one left."

So he took out the second citron, cut it in two, and lo, a maiden twice as beautiful as the first stood before him. She bowed low and said:

"Have you food ready for me? Have you drink

ready for me? Have you pretty clothes ready for me?"

"No, lovely creature, I haven't! I haven't!"

The maiden clapped her hands thrice, bowed before him, and disappeared.

Now there was only one citron left. The prince took it in his hand, looked at it, and said: "I won't cut you open until I'm safe at home in my father's house."

He took up his journey again and on the third day he came to his native town and his father's castle. He had been gone a long time and how he ever got back he didn't know himself.

Tears of joy rained down the old king's cheeks.

"Welcome home, my son, welcome a hundred times!" he cried, falling on the prince's neck.

The prince related the adventures of his journey and they at home told him how anxiously they had awaited his return.

On the next day a great feast was prepared. All the nobles in the land were invited. The tables were spread with food and drink the most expensive in the world and many rich dresses embroidered in gold and studded with pearls were laid out.

The guests assembled, seated themselves at the

tables, and waited. Music played and when all was ready, the prince took the last citron and cut it in two. Out jumped a beautiful creature, three times lovelier than the others.

" Have you food ready for me? " she cried. " Have you drink ready for me? Have you pretty clothes ready for me? "

" I have indeed, dear heart! " the prince answered. " I have everything ready for you! "

He led her to the gorgeous clothes and she dressed herself in them and every one present marveled at her great beauty.

Soon the betrothal took place and after the betrothal a magnificent wedding.

So now the old king's wish was fulfilled. He blessed his son, gave over the kingdom to him, and not long afterwards he died.

The first thing that faced the young king after his father's death was a war which a neighboring king stirred up against him. So the young king had to bid farewell to the bride whom he had won so dearly and lead his men to battle. In order that nothing happen to the queen in his absence, he built a golden throne for her in the garden beside the lake. This throne was as high as a tower and no one could ascend

Music Played

it except those to whom the queen let down a silken cord.

Not far from the king's castle lived the old woman who, in the first place, had told him about the Three Citrons. She knew well enough how the young king had won his bride and she was deeply incensed that he had not invited her to the wedding and in fact had not even thanked her for her good advice.

Now this old woman had a gipsy for servant whom she used to send to the lake for water. One day when this gipsy was filling her pitcher, she saw in the lake a beautiful reflection. She supposed it was a reflection of herself.

" Is it right," she cried out, " that so lovely a creature as I should carry water for that old witch? "

In a fury she threw the pitcher on the ground and broke it into a hundred pieces. Then she looked up and discovered that it wasn't her own reflection she had seen in the water but that of the beautiful queen.

Ashamed of herself, she picked up the broken pitcher and went home. The old woman, who knew beforehand what had happened, went out to meet her with a new pitcher.

" It's no matter about the pitcher," the old woman said. " Go back to the lake and beg the lovely lady to let down the silken cord and pull you up. Tell her you will comb her hair. When she pulls you up, comb her hair until she falls asleep. Then stick this pin into her head. After that you can dress yourself up in her clothes and sit there like a queen."

It was easy enough to persuade the gipsy. She took the pitcher and the pin and returned to the lake.

As she drew water she gazed at the lovely queen.

" Oh, how beautiful you are! " she whined, leering up at the queen with an evil eye. " How beautiful you are! Aye, but you'd be a hundred times more beautiful if you but let me comb out your lovely hair! Indeed, I would so twine those golden tresses that your lord would be delighted! "

With words like these she beguiled and coaxed the queen until she let down the silken cord and drew the gipsy up. Once on the throne, the wicked gipsy combed out the golden tresses and plaited them and arranged them until the queen fell sound asleep. Then the gipsy took the pin and stuck it into the queen's head. Instantly a beautiful white dove flew off the golden throne and not a trace was left of the lovely queen except her rich clothing. The gipsy dressed herself in this, sat in the queen's place, and gazed down into the lake. But in the lake no lovely reflection showed itself, for even in the queen's clothes the gipsy remained a gipsy.

The young king waged a successful war against his enemies and made peace. Scarcely had he got home when he hurried to the garden to see whether anything had happened to his heart's delight. Who can express in words his astonishment and horror when instead of his beautiful wife he saw the evil gipsy!

"Ah, my dearest one, how you have changed!" he murmured and tears flowed down his cheeks.

"Yes, my dear, I have changed, I know I have," the gipsy answered. "It was grief for you that has broken me."

She tried to fall on his neck but the king turned quickly away and left her.

From that time forth he had no peace but day and night he mourned the lost beauty of his wife and nothing consoled him.

Grieving in this way and thinking always the same sad thoughts, he was walking one day in the garden when suddenly a beautiful white dove flew down from a high tree and alighted on his hand. She looked up at him with eyes as mournful as his own.

"Ah, my poor dove," the king said, "why are you so sad? Has your mate also changed?"

As he spoke he stroked the dove gently on the back and on the head. On the head he felt a little lump. He blew aside the feathers and discovered the head of a pin. He pulled out the pin and instantly the sad dove changed into his own beautiful wife.

She told him what had happened to her, how the gipsy had deceived her and stuck the pin into her head. The king had the gipsy and the old witch caught at once and burnt at the stake.

From that time on nothing happened to mar the king's happiness, neither the plots of his enemies nor the spite of evil people. He lived in love and peace with his beautiful wife and he ruled his kingdom wisely. In fact he's ruling it still if he hasn't died.

PRINCE BAYAYA

THE STORY OF A MAGIC HORSE

PRINCE BAYAYA

WHILE the king of a distant country was off at the wars, his wife, the queen, gave birth to twin sons. There was great rejoicing throughout the court and immediately messengers were despatched to the king to carry him news of the happy event.

Both boys were well and vigorous and shot up like little trees. The one who was about a moment the older was the hardier of the two. Even as a toddling child he was forever playing in the courtyard and struggling to climb on the back of a horse that had been given him because it was just his own age.

His brother, on the other hand, liked better to play indoors on the soft carpets. He was always tagging after his mother and never went outdoors except when he followed the queen into the garden. For this reason the younger prince became the mother's favorite.

The boys were seven years old before the king returned from the wars. He looked at his sons with pride and joy and he said to the queen:

" But which is the older and which is the younger? "

The queen, thinking that the king was asking in order to know which was the heir to the throne, slipped in her favorite as the older. The king, of course, did not question his wife's word and so, thereafter, he always spoke of the younger one as his heir.

When the boys had grown into handsome youths, the older one wearied of life at home and of hearing his brother always spoken of as the future king. He longed to go out into the world and seek adventures of his own. One day as he was pouring out his heart to the little horse that had been his companion from infancy, much to his amazement the horse spoke to him with a human voice and said:

" Since you are not happy at home, go out into the world. But do not go without your father's permission. I advise you to take no one with you and to mount no horse but me. This will bring you good luck."

The prince asked the horse how it happened that he could talk like a human being.

" Don't ask me about that," the horse said, " for I can't tell you. But I wish to be your friend and counselor and I will be as long as you obey me."

The prince promised to do as the horse advised. He went at once to his father to beg his leave to ride

When the Boys Had Grown into Handsome Youths

out into the world. At first his father was unwilling to let him go but his mother gave her permission at once. By dint of coaxing he finally won his father's consent. Of course the king wanted the prince to set forth in a manner befitting his rank with a great company of men and horses. But the prince insisted that he wished to go unattended.

"Why, my dear father, do I need any such retinue as you suggest? Let me have some money for the journey and let me ride off alone on my own little horse. This will give me more freedom and less trouble."

Again he had to argue with his father for some time, but at last he succeeded in arranging everything to his liking.

The day of parting came. The little horse stood saddled at the castle gate. The prince bade farewell to his parents and his brother. They all wept on his neck and at the last moment the queen's heart misgave her for the deceit she had practised and she made the prince solemnly promise that he would return home within a year or at least send them word of his whereabouts.

So the prince mounted his little horse and off they trotted. The horse went at a surprising pace for an animal that was seventeen years old, but of course you have guessed before this that he was no ordinary horse. The years had not touched him at all. His coat was as smooth as satin and his legs were straight and sound. No matter how far he traveled he was always as fresh as a fawn.

He carried the prince a great distance until they came in sight of the towers of a beautiful city. Then the horse left the beaten track and crossed a field to a big rock.

When they reached the rock, the horse kicked it with his hoof three times and the rock opened. They rode inside and the prince found himself in a comfortable stable.

"Now you will leave me here," the horse said, "and go on alone to the nearby town. You must pretend you are dumb and be careful never to betray yourself. Present yourself at court and have the king take you into his service. When you need anything, no matter what it is, come to the rock, knock three times, and the rock will open to you."

The prince thought to himself: " My horse certainly knows what he's about, so of course I'll do exactly as he says."

He disguised himself by bandaging one eye and

making his face look pale and sallow. Then he presented himself at court and the king, pitying his youth and his affliction of dumbness, took him into his service.

The prince was capable and quick at affairs and it wasn't long before the king gave over to him the management of the household. His advice was asked in matters of importance and all day long he hurried about the castle going from one thing to another. If the king needed a scribe, there wasn't a cleverer one anywhere than the prince. Everybody liked him and everybody was soon calling him Bayaya, because those were the only sounds he made.

The king had three daughters, each more beautiful than the other. The oldest was called Zdobena, the second Budinka, and the youngest Slavena.

The prince loved to be with the three girls and as he was supposed to be dumb and in his disguise was very ugly, the king made no objection to his spending his days with them. How could the king possibly think that there was any danger of Bayaya's stealing the heart of one of the princesses? They liked him, all three of them, and were always taking him with them wherever they went. He wove garlands for them, spun golden thread, picked them flowers, and drew them designs of birds and flowers for their embroidery. He liked them all, but he liked the youngest one best. Everything he did for her was done a little better than for the others. The garlands he wove her were richer, the designs he drew for her were more beautiful. The two older sisters noticed this and laughed, and when they were alone they teased Slavena. Slavena, who had a sweet and amiable disposition, accepted their joking without retort.

Bayaya had been at the court some time when one morning he found the king sitting sad and gloomy over his breakfast. So by signs he asked him what was the matter.

The king looked at him and sighed. " Is it possible, my dear boy," he said, " that you don't know what's the matter? Don't you know the calamity that threatens us? Don't you know the bitter three days that are at hand for me? "

Bayaya, alarmed by the seriousness of the king's manner, shook his head.

" Then I'll tell you," said the king, " although you can be of no help. Years ago three dragons came flying through the air and alighted on a great rock near here. The first was nine-headed, the second eighteen-headed, and the third twenty-seven-headed. At once they laid waste the country, devouring the cattle and killing the people. Soon the city was in a state of siege. To keep them away we placed all the food we had outside the gates and in a short time we ourselves were starving. In desperation I had an old wise woman called to court and asked her was there any way to drive these monsters from the land. Alas for me, there was a way and that way was to promise the awful creatures my three beautiful daughters when they reached womanhood. At that time my daughters were only small children and I thought to myself many things might happen in the years before they grew up. So, to relieve my stricken land, I promised the dragons my daughters. The poor queen died at once of grief, but my daughters grew up knowing nothing of their fate. As soon as I made the monstrous bargain, the dragons flew away and until yesterday were never again heard of. Last night, a shepherd, beside himself with terror, brought me the news that the dragons are again settled in their old rock and are sending out fearful roars. Tomorrow I must sacrifice to them my oldest child, the day after tomorrow my second child, and the day after that my youngest. Then I shall be left a poor lonely old man with nothing."

The king strode up and down and tore his hair in grief.

In great distress Bayaya went to the princesses. He found them dressed in black and looking ghastly pale. They were sitting in a row and bewailing their fate most piteously. Bayaya tried to comfort them, telling them by signs that surely some one would appear to rescue them. But they paid no heed to him and kept on moaning and weeping.

Grief and confusion spread throughout the city, for every one loved the royal family. Every house as well as the palace was soon draped in black and the sound of mourning was heard on every side.

Bayaya hurried secretly out of the city and across the field to the rock where his magic horse was stabled. He knocked three times, the rock opened, and he entered.

He stroked the horse's shining mane and kissed his muzzle in greeting.

"My dear horse," he said, "I have come to you for advice. Help me and I shall be happy forever."

So he told the horse the story of the dragons.

"Oh, I know all about those dragons," the horse answered. "In fact, it was that you might rescue the princesses that I brought you here in the first place.

Early tomorrow morning come back and I will tell you
what to do."

Bayaya returned to the castle with such joy shining in his face that if any one had noticed him he
would have been severely rebuked. He spent the day
with the princesses trying to comfort and console them,
but in spite of all he could do they felt only more terrified as the hours went by.

The next day at the first streak of dawn he was at
the rock.

The horse greeted him and said: " Lift up the
stone under my trough and take out what you find
there."

Bayaya obeyed. He lifted the stone and under the
stone he found a large chest. Inside the chest he found
three beautiful suits of clothing, with caps and plumes
to match, a sword, and a horse's bridle. The first
suit was red embroidered in silver and studded with
diamonds, the second was pure white embroidered in
gold, and the third was light blue richly embroidered
with silver and studded with diamonds and pearls.

For all three suits there was but one mighty sword.
Its blade was beautifully inlaid and its scabbard shone
with precious stones. The horse's bridle was also richly
jeweled.

"All three suits are for you," the horse said. "For the first day, put on the red one."

So Bayaya dressed himself in the red suit, buckled on his sword, and threw the bridle over the horse's head.

"Have no fear," the horse said as they left the rock. "Cut bravely into the monster, trusting to your sword. And remember, do not dismount."

At the castle heart-broken farewells were being taken. Zdobena parted from her father and her sisters, stepped into a carriage, and accompanied by a great multitude of her weeping subjects was slowly driven out of town to the Dragon Rock. As they neared the fatal spot the princess alighted. She took a few steps forward, then sank to the earth in a faint.

At that moment the people saw galloping toward them a knight with a red and white plume. In a voice of authority he ordered them to stand back and leave him to deal alone with the dragon. They were glad enough to lead the princess away and they all went to a hill near by from which they could watch the combat at a safe distance.

Now there was a deep rumbling noise, the earth shook, and the Dragon Rock opened. A nine-headed monster crawled out. He spat fire and poison from

all his nine mouths and cast about his nine heads, this
way and that, looking for his promised prey.   When
he saw the knight he let out a horrible roar.

Bayaya rode straight at him and with one blow of
his sword cut off three of his heads.   The dragon
writhed and enveloped Bayaya in flames and poisonous
fumes.   But the prince, undaunted, struck at him again
and again until he had cut off all nine heads.   The
life that still remained in the loathsome body, the horse
finished with his hoofs.

When the dragon had perished the prince turned
and galloped back the way he had come.

Zdobena looked after him, wishing she might follow
him to thank him for her deliverance.   But she remembered her poor father sunk in grief at the castle
and she felt it was her duty to hurry back to him as
quickly as she could.

It would be impossible to describe in words the
king's joy when Zdobena appeared before him safe
and uninjured.   Her sisters embraced her and wondered for the first time whether a deliverer would rise
up for them as well.

Bayaya capered happily about and assured them
by signs that he was certain they, too, would be saved.
Although the prospect of the morrow still terrified

them, yet hope had come to them and once or twice Bayaya succeeded in making them laugh.

The next day Budinka was led out. As on the day before, the unknown knight appeared, this time wearing a white plume. He attacked the eighteen-headed dragon and, after valiant conflict, despatched him. Then before any one could reach him, he turned and rode away.

The princess returned to the castle, grieving that she had not been able to speak to the knight and express her gratitude.

"You, my sisters," Slavena said, "were backward not to speak to him before he rode off. Tomorrow if he delivers me I shall kneel before him and not get up until he consents to return with me to the castle."

Just then Bayaya began laughing and chuckling and Slavena asked him sharply what was the matter. He capered about and made her understand that he, too, wanted to see the knight.

On the third day Slavena was taken out to the Dragon Rock. This time the king also went. The heart of the poor girl quaked with terror when she thought that if the unknown knight failed to appear she would be handed over to the horrible monster.

A joyous shout from the people told her that the

knight was coming. Then she saw him, a gallant figure in blue with a blue and white plume floating in the wind. As he had killed the first dragon, and the second dragon, so he killed the third although the struggle was longer and the little horse had much to do to stand up against the poisonous fumes.

Instantly the dragon was slain, Slavena and the king rushed up to the knight and begged him to return with them to the castle. He scarcely knew how to refuse, especially when Slavena, kneeling before him, grasped the edge of his tunic and looked up at him so bewitchingly that his heart melted and he was ready to do anything she asked.

But the little horse took matters into his own hands, reared up suddenly, and galloped off before the knight had time to dismount.

So Slavena, too, was unable to bring the knight back to the castle. The king and all the court were greatly disappointed but their disappointment was swallowed up in their joy that the princesses had been so miraculously saved.

Shortly after this another disaster threatened the king. A neighboring king of great power declared war against him. The king sent far and wide and summoned together all the nobles of the land. They came, and the king when he had laid before them his cause promised them the hands of his three beautiful daughters in return for their support. This was indeed an inducement and every young noble present swore his allegiance and hurried home to gather his forces.

Troops poured in from all sides and soon the king was ready to set forth.

He handed over the affairs of the castle to Bayaya and also intrusted to him the safety of the three princesses. Bayaya did his duty faithfully, looking after the castle and planning diversions for the princesses to keep them happy and cheerful.

Then one day he complained of feeling sick, but instead of consulting the court physician, he said he would go himself to the fields and hunt some herbs. The princesses laughed at his whim but let him go.

He hurried to the rock where his horse was stabled, knocked three times, and entered.

" You have come in good time," the horse said. " The king's forces are weakening and tomorrow will decide the battle. Put on the white suit, take your sword, and let us be off."

Bayaya kissed his brave little horse and put on his white suit.

That night the king was awake planning the morrow's battle and sending swift messengers to his daughters instructing them what to do in case the day went against him.

The next morning as the battle joined an unknown knight suddenly appeared among the king's forces. He was all in white. He rode a little horse and he wielded a mighty sword.

He struck right and left among the enemy and he caused such havoc that the king's forces were instantly heartened. Gathering around the white knight they fought so valiantly that soon the enemy broke and scattered and the king won a mighty victory.

The knight himself was slightly wounded on the foot. When the king saw this he jumped down from his horse, tore off a piece of his own cape, and bound up the wound. He begged the knight to dismount and come with him to a tent. But the knight, thanking him, refused, spurred his horse, and was gone.

The king nearly wept with disappointment that the unknown knight to whom he was under one more obligation had again ridden off without so much as leaving his name.

With great rejoicing the king's forces marched home carrying vast stores of booty.

"Well, steward," said the king to Bayaya, "how have the affairs of the household gone in my absence?"

Bayaya nodded that everything had gone well, but the princesses laughed at him and Slavena said:

"I must enter complaint against your steward, for he was disobedient. He said he was sick but he would not consult the court physician. He said he wanted to go himself and get some herbs. He went and he was gone two whole days and when he came back he was sicker than before."

The king looked at Bayaya to see if he was still sick. Bayaya shook his head and capered about to show the king that he was all right.

When the princesses heard that the unknown knight had again appeared and saved the day they were unwilling to become at once the brides of any of the nobles, for they thought the knight might perhaps come demanding one of them.

Again the king was in a quandary. All the various nobles had helped him valiantly and the question now arose to what three of them would the princesses be awarded. After much thought the king hit upon a plan which he hoped would decide the matter to the satisfaction of them all. He called a meeting of the nobles and said:

"My dear comrades in arms, you remember that I promised the hands of my daughters to those of you who would support me in battle. All of you gave me valiant support. Each of you deserves the hand of one of my daughters. But, alas, I have only three daughters. To decide therefore which three of you my daughters shall marry I make this suggestion: let all of you stand in the garden in a row and let each of my daughters throw down a golden apple from a balcony. Then each princess must wed the man to whom her apple rolls. My lords, do you all agree to this?"

The nobles all agreed and the king sent for his daughters. The princesses, still thinking of the unknown knight, were not enthusiastic over this arrangement, but not to shame their father they, too, agreed.

So each of the girls, dressed in her loveliest, took a golden apple in her hand and went up to a balcony.

Below in the garden the nobles stood in a row. Bayaya, as though he were a spectator, took his place at the end of the line.

First Zdobena threw down her apple. It rolled straight to the feet of Bayaya but he turned quickly aside and it rolled on to a handsome youth who snatched it up with joy and stepped from the line.

Then Budinka threw her apple. It, too, rolled to Bayaya but he cleverly kicked it on so that it seemed to roll straight to the feet of a valiant lord who picked it up and then looked with happy eyes at his lovely bride.

Last Slavena threw her apple. This time Bayaya did not step aside but when the apple rolled to him he stooped and picked it up. Then he ran to the balcony, knelt before the princess, and kissed her hand.

Slavena snatched away her hand and ran to her chamber, where she wept bitterly to think she would have to marry Bayaya instead of the unknown knight.

The king was much disappointed and the nobles murmured. But what was done was done, and could not be undone.

That night there was a great feast but Slavena remained in her chamber refusing to appear among the guests.

It was moonlight and from the rock in the field the little horse carried his master for the last time. When they reached the castle Bayaya dismounted. Then he kissed his faithful friend farewell, and the little horse vanished.

Slavena still sat in her chamber, sad and unhappy. When a maidservant opened the door and said that

Bayaya wished to speak to her, the princess hid her face in the pillows.

Presently some one took her by the hand and when she raised her head she saw standing before her the beautiful knight of her dreams.

" Are you angry with your bridegroom that you hide from him? " he asked.

" Why do you ask me that? " Slavena whispered. " You are not my bridegroom. Bayaya is my bride-groom."

" I am Bayaya. I am the dumb youth who wove you garlands. I am the knight who saved you and your sisters from death and who helped your father in battle. See, here is the piece of your father's cape with which he bound up my wounded foot."

That this was so was joy indeed to Slavena. She led the white knight into the banquet hall and presented him to the king as her bridegroom. When all had been explained, the king rejoiced, the guests marveled, and Zdobena and Budinka looked sideways at each other with little gasps of envy.

After the wedding Bayaya rode away with Slavena to visit his parents. When he reached his native town the first news he got was of the death of his brother. He hurried to the castle to comfort his parents. They were overjoyed at his return, for they had long ago given him up for dead.

After a time Bayaya succeeded to the kingdom. He lived long and prospered and he enjoyed unclouded happiness with his wife.

KATCHA AND THE DEVIL

THE STORY OF A CLINGING VINE

KATCHA AND THE DEVIL

THERE was once a woman named Katcha who lived in a village where she owned her own cottage and garden. She had money besides but little good it did her because she was such an ill-tempered vixen that nobody, not even the poorest laborer, would marry her. Nobody would even work for her, no matter what she paid, for she couldn't open her mouth without scolding, and whenever she scolded she raised her shrill voice until you could hear it a mile away. The older she grew the worse she became until by the time she was forty she was as sour as vinegar.

Now as it always happens in a village, every Sunday afternoon there was a dance either at the burgomaster's, or at the tavern. As soon as the bagpipes sounded, the boys all crowded into the room and the girls gathered outside and looked in the windows. Katcha was always the first at the window. The music would strike up and the boys would beckon the girls to come in and dance, but no one ever beckoned Katcha.

Even when she paid the piper no one ever asked her to dance. Yet she came Sunday after Sunday just the same.

One Sunday afternoon as she was hurrying to the tavern she thought to herself: " Here I am getting old and yet I've never once danced with a boy! Plague take it, today I'd dance with the devil if he asked me! "

She was in a fine rage by the time she reached the tavern, where she sat down near the stove and looked around to see what girls the boys had invited to dance.

Suddenly a stranger in hunter's green came in. He sat down at a table near Katcha and ordered drink. When the serving maid brought the beer, he reached over to Katcha and asked her to drink with him. At first she was much taken back at this attention, then she pursed her lips coyly and pretended to refuse, but finally she accepted.

When they had finished drinking, he pulled a ducat from his pocket, tossed it to the piper, and called out:

" Clear the floor, boys! This is for Katcha and me alone! "

The boys snickered and the girls giggled hiding behind each other and stuffing their aprons into their mouths so that Katcha wouldn't hear them laughing. But Katcha wasn't noticing them at all. Katcha was dancing with a fine young man! If the whole world had been laughing at her, Katcha wouldn't have cared.

The stranger danced with Katcha all afternoon and all evening. Not once did he dance with any one else. He bought her marzipan and sweet drinks and, when the hour came to go home, he escorted her through the village.

" Ah," sighed Katcha when they reached her cottage and it was time to part, " I wish I could dance with you forever! "

" Very well," said the stranger. " Come with me."

" Where do you live? "

" Put your arm around my neck and I'll tell you."

Katcha put both arms about his neck and instantly the man changed into a devil and flew straight down to hell.

At the gates of hell he stopped and knocked.

His comrades came and opened the gates and when they saw that he was exhausted, they tried to take Katcha off his neck. But Katcha held on tight and nothing they could do or say would make her budge.

The devil finally had to appear before the Prince of Darkness himself with Katcha still glued to his neck.

" What's that thing you've got around your neck? " the Prince asked.

So the devil told how as he was walking about on earth he had heard Katcha say she would dance with the devil himself if he asked her. " So I asked her to dance with me," the devil said. " Afterwards just to frighten her a little I brought her down to hell. And now she won't let go of me!"

" Serve you right, you dunce!" the Prince said. " How often have I told you to use common sense when you go wandering around on earth! You might have known Katcha would never let go of a man once she had him!"

" I beg your Majesty to make her let go!" the poor devil implored.

" I will not!" said the Prince. " You'll have to carry her back to earth yourself and get rid of her as best you can. Perhaps this will be a lesson to you."

So the devil, very tired and very cross, shambled back to earth with Katcha still clinging to his neck. He tried every way to get her off. He promised her wooded hills and rich meadows if she but let him go. He cajoled her, he cursed her, but all to no avail. Katcha still held on.

Breathless and discouraged he came at last to a meadow where a shepherd, wrapped in a great shaggy sheepskin coat, was tending his flocks. The devil transformed himself into an ordinary looking man so that the shepherd didn't recognize him.

" Hi, there," the shepherd said, " what's that you're carrying? "

" Don't ask me," the devil said with a sigh. " I'm so worn out I'm nearly dead. I was walking yonder not thinking of anything at all when along comes a woman and jumps on my back and won't let go. I'm trying to carry her to the nearest village to get rid of her there, but I don't believe I'm able. My legs are giving out."

The shepherd, who was a good-natured chap, said: " I tell you what: I'll help you. I can't leave my sheep long, but I'll carry her halfway."

" Oh," said the devil, " I'd be very grateful if you did! "

So the shepherd yelled at Katcha: " Hi, there, you! Catch hold of me! "

When Katcha saw that the shepherd was a handsome youth, she let go of the devil and leapt upon the shepherd's back, catching hold of the collar of his sheepskin coat.

Now the young shepherd soon found that the long shaggy coat and Katcha made a pretty heavy load for walking. In a few moments he was sick of his bargain and began casting about for some way of getting rid of Katcha.

Presently he came to a pond and he thought to himself that he'd like to throw her in. He wondered how he could do it. Perhaps he could manage it by throwing in his greatcoat with her. The coat was so loose that he thought he could slip out of it without Katcha's discovering what he was doing. Very cautiously he slipped out one arm. Katcha didn't move. He slipped out the other arm. Still Katcha didn't move. He unlooped the first button. Katcha noticed nothing. He unlooped the second button. Still Katcha noticed nothing. He unlooped the third button and kerplunk! he had pitched coat and Katcha and all into the middle of the pond!

When he got back to his sheep, the devil looked at him in amazement.

" Where's Katcha? " he gasped.

" Oh," the shepherd said, pointing over his shoulder with his thumb, " I decided to leave her up yonder in a pond."

" My dear friend," the devil cried, " I thank you! You have done me a great favor. If it hadn't been for you I might be carrying Katcha till doomsday. I'll never forget you and some time I'll reward you.

As you don't know who it is you've helped, I must tell you I'm a devil."

With these words the devil vanished.

For a moment the shepherd was dazed. Then he laughed and said to himself: " Well, if they're all as stupid as he is, we ought to be able for them! "

The country where the shepherd lived was ruled over by a dissolute young duke who passed his days in riotous living and his nights in carousing. He gave over the affairs of state to two governors who were as bad as he. With extortionate taxes and unjust fines they robbed the people until the whole land was crying out against them.

Now one day for amusement the duke summoned an astrologer to court and ordered him to read in the planets the fate of himself and his two governors. When the astrologer had cast a horoscope for each of the three reprobates, he was greatly disturbed and tried to dissuade the duke from questioning him further.

" Such danger," he said, " threatens your life and the lives of your two governors that I fear to speak."

" Whatever it is," said the duke, " speak. But I warn you to speak the truth, for if what you say does not come to pass you will forfeit your life."

The astrologer bowed and said: " Hear then, oh Duke, what the planets foretell: Before the second quarter of the moon, on such and such a day, at such and such an hour, a devil will come and carry off the two governors. At the full of the moon on such and such a day, at such and such an hour, the same devil will come for your Highness and carry you off to hell."

The duke pretended to be unconcerned but in his heart he was deeply shaken. The voice of the astrologer sounded to him like the voice of judgment and for the first time conscience began to trouble him.

As for the governors, they couldn't eat a bite of food and were carried from the palace half dead with fright. They piled their ill-gotten wealth into wagons and rode away to their castles, where they barred all the doors and windows in order to keep the devil out.

The duke reformed. He gave up his evil ways and corrected the abuses of state in the hope of averting if possible his cruel fate.

The poor shepherd had no inkling of any of these things. He tended his flocks from day to day and never bothered his head about the happenings in the great world.

Suddenly one day the devil appeared before him

and said: " I have come, my friend, to repay you for your kindness. When the moon is in its first quarter, 'I was to carry off the former governors of this land because they robbed the poor and gave the duke evil counsel. However, they're behaving themselves now so they're to be given another chance. But they don't know this. Now on such and such a day do you go to the first castle where a crowd of people will be assembled. When a cry goes up and the gates open and I come dragging out the governor, do you step up to me and say: ' What do you mean by this? Get out of here or there'll be trouble!' I'll pretend to be greatly frightened and make off. Then ask the governor to pay you two bags of gold, and if he haggles just threaten to call me back. After that go on to the castle of the second governor and do the same thing and demand the same pay. I warn you, though, be prudent with the money and use it only for good. When the moon is full, I'm to carry off the duke himself, for he was so wicked that he's to have no second chance. So don't try to save him, for if you do you'll pay for it with your own skin. Don't forget! "

The shepherd remembered carefully everything the devil told him. When the moon was in its first quarter he went to the first castle. A great crowd of people was gathered outside waiting to see the devil carry away the governor.

Suddenly there was a loud cry of despair, the gates of the castle opened, and there was the devil, as black as night, dragging out the governor. He, poor man, was half dead with fright.

The shepherd elbowed his way through the crowd, took the governor by the hand, and pushed the devil roughly aside.

"What do you mean by this?" he shouted. "Get out of here or there'll be trouble!"

Instantly the devil fled and the governor fell on his knees before the shepherd and kissed his hands and begged him to state what he wanted in reward. When the shepherd asked for two bags of gold, the governor ordered that they be given him without delay.

Then the shepherd went to the castle of the second governor and went through exactly the same performance.

It goes without saying that the duke soon heard of the shepherd, for he had been anxiously awaiting the fate of the two governors. At once he sent a wagon with four horses to fetch the shepherd to the palace and when the shepherd arrived he begged him piteously to rescue him likewise from the devil's clutches.

" Master," the shepherd answered, " I cannot promise you anything. I have to consider my own safety. You have been a great sinner, but if you really want to reform, if you really want to rule your people justly and kindly and wisely as becomes a true ruler, then indeed I will help you even if I have to suffer hellfire in your place."

The duke declared that with God's help he would mend his ways and the shepherd promised to come back on the fatal day.

With grief and dread the whole country awaited the coming of the full moon. In the first place the people had greeted the astrologer's prophecy with joy, but since the duke had reformed their feelings for him had changed.

Time sped fast as time does whether joy be coming or sorrow and all too soon the fatal day arrived.

Dressed in black and pale with fright, the duke sat expecting the arrival of the devil.

Suddenly the door flew open and the devil, black as night, stood before him. He paused a moment and then he said, politely:

" Your time has come, Lord Duke, and I am here to get you! "

Without a word the duke arose and followed the

devil to the courtyard, which was filled with a great multitude of people.

At that moment the shepherd, all out of breath, came pushing his way through the crowd, and ran straight at the devil, shouting out:

"What do you mean by this? Get out of here or there'll be trouble!"

"What do *you* mean?" whispered the devil. "Don't you remember what I told you?"

"Hush!" the shepherd whispered back. "I don't care anything about the duke. This is to warn you! You know Katcha? She's alive and she's looking for you!"

The instant the devil heard the name of Katcha he turned and fled.

All the people cheered the shepherd, while the shepherd himself laughed in his sleeve to think that he had taken in the devil so easily.

As for the duke, he was so grateful to the shepherd 'that he made him his chief counselor and loved him as a brother. And well he might, for the shepherd was a sensible man and always gave him sound advice.

THE BETROTHAL GIFTS

THE STORY OF KUBIK AND THE FROG

THE BETROTHAL GIFTS

A FARMER who had three sons was much troubled in his mind as to how he should leave his property. "My farm is too small to divide," he kept thinking to himself. "If I divide it into three equal parts and give each of my sons one part, they will all be poor cottagers, and yet, if I give it all to one son, I shall be unjust to the other two. My grandfather always said that it is a father's duty to treat all his children alike and I'm sure I don't want to depart from his teachings."

At last he called his sons together and said: "I have hit upon a plan whereby fate shall decide which of you shall be my heir. You must all go out into the world and find brides, and he who brings back as a betrothal gift the most beautiful ring shall have the farm."

The sons agreed to this plan and the next day they all set out in different directions in quest of brides.

Now the youngest son, whose name was Kubik, was

not considered as bright as his brothers, for he was kind to beggars and he never drove a hard bargain. His brothers often laughed at him and his father pitied him, for he thought that Kubik was too gentle to make his way in the world.

Kubik's path took him into a deep forest. He walked on and on until suddenly a little frog hopped up in front of him and said:

"Where are you going, Kubik?"

Now Kubik had never in all his life heard of a frog that could talk. At first he was frightened but even so he was too polite not to answer a civil question. So he told the frog about his father and the farm and the quest for betrothal gifts upon which he and his brothers were bound.

The frog listened and when he was finished she said: "Come with me, Kubik, and my daughter, Kachenka, will give you a more beautiful ring than any your father or brothers have ever seen."

Kubik hesitated, but at last not to hurt the frog's feelings he agreed. "But if your daughter Kachenka looks like you," he thought to himself, "Heaven help me, for she'll be a pretty dear price to pay for a farm!"

The frog led him to a deep valley at one side of which rose a high rocky cliff that was honey-combed with caverns. The frog hopped into one of these and called out:

"Kachenka, my child, where are you? Here is Kubik come to woo you and to beg a betrothal gift. Bring out your little box of rings."

Instantly a second frog appeared dragging a heavy jewel casket. Kachenka, alas, was a hundred times uglier than her mother. Her legs were crooked, her face was all covered with spots, and when she spoke her voice was hoarse and croaking.

For a moment Kubik shivered and turned away in disgust, but only for a moment until he remembered that it wasn't Kachenka's fault that she was a frog.

The two frogs put the casket before him and opened it and Kubik saw that it was filled with a collection of the rarest and most beautiful rings in the world.

"Make your own choice, Kubik," the old frog said.

Kubik selected as plain a ring as there was, for he was ashamed to take one of the handsomest.

"Not that one!" the old frog said, "unless you want your brothers to laugh at you."

Thereupon she herself picked out the ring that had the biggest diamond of them all, wrapped it up carefully in paper, and handed it to Kubik.

"Now hurry home," she said, "for your brothers

are already there and your father is waiting for you."

As soon as Kubik reached home the farmer called his three sons together and demanded to be shown their betrothal gifts.

All the eldest son had was a common brass ring.

"Um," the farmer said, shaking his head. ",Well, put it away for a keepsake."

The second son showed a silver ring that was worth a few cents more.

"A little better," the old man mumbled, "but not good enough for a farmer. Put it away for a keepsake. And now," he said, turning to his youngest son, "let us see what Kubik has brought from his promised bride."

They all looked at Kubik, and Kubik blushed as he felt in his pocket for the little package.

"Ho, ho!" his brothers laughed. "Kubik has such a fine ring that he has to keep it wrapped up."

But when he opened the paper they stopped laughing, and well they might, for there was a great diamond that sparkled and blazed until it seemed that the sun was shining in the room.

"Kubik!" the farmer cried when at last he found his voice, "where did you get that ring? You must have stolen it, you wicked boy!" And without waiting to hear what Kubik had to say, he reached for a whip and trounced the poor lad to within an inch of his life. Then he took the ring and hid it carefully away.

" Now, my boys," he said to his sons, " you will all have to make another trial. This time ask of your promised brides the gift of an embroidered kerchief and he who brings back the most beautiful kerchief shall be my heir."

So the next day the three sons again started out, each in a different direction.

Kubik thought to himself: " I won't go the way I went yesterday or I may meet that old frog again and then, when I get home, the only prize I'll get will be another beating."

So he took a different path but he hadn't gone far before the old frog hopped up in front of him.

" What's the matter, Kubik? " she asked.

At first Kubik didn't want to tell her but she questioned him and finally, not to seem rude, he told her about the beating his father had given him on account of Kachenka's ring and about the new quest for embroidered kerchiefs upon which his father was now sending him and his brothers.

" Now don't think any more about that whipping," the old frog advised him. " And as for an embroidered kerchief, why, Kachenka is the very girl for that! She will give you one that will make your brothers open their eyes!"

Kubik wasn't sure that he wanted to accept another of Kachenka's gifts, but the old frog urged him and at last he agreed. So again they took the path to the rocky cliff. The old frog called her daughter out as before and presently Kachenka appeared dragging a chest that was filled with the most wonderful of kerchiefs, all of fine silk and all richly embroidered and so large that they were more like shawls than kerchiefs.

Kubik reached in and took the first that came to hand.

"Tut, tut!" the old frog said. "That's no way to select a kerchief."

Then she herself picked out the biggest and the most richly embroidered of them all and wrapped it up in paper. She gave it to Kubik and said:

"Now hurry home, for your brothers are already there and your father is waiting for you."

As soon as Kubik reached home the farmer called his three sons together and demanded to be shown their betrothal gifts.

All the eldest one had was a small cheap kerchief of no value whatever.

"Um," the farmer said, shaking his head. "Well, put it away for a keepsake."

The kerchief of the second had cost a few cents more.

"A little better," the old man mumbled. "Perhaps it's good enough for a farmer. And now," he said, turning to his youngest son, "let us see what Kubik has brought from his promised bride."

They all looked at Kubik, and Kubik blushed as he pulled out a parcel from under his shirt.

"Ho, ho!" his brothers laughed. "Kubik has such a fine kerchief that he has to keep it wrapped up in paper!"

But when Kubik opened the paper they stopped laughing, and well they might, for there was a silken kerchief so big that it could have covered the whole room and so richly embroidered that any princess in the world would have been proud to own it.

"Kubik!" the farmer cried when at last he was able to speak, "where did you get that kerchief? You must have stolen it, you wicked boy!" And without waiting to hear what Kubik had to say, he reached down the whip again and trounced the poor boy to within an inch of his life. Then he took the kerchief and hid it carefully away.

"Now, my sons," he said, "you will all have to make another trial. But this time it will not be for a ring or a kerchief. This time bring home your brides and he whose bride is the most beautiful shall be my heir."

So the next day the three sons again started out, each in a different direction.

"I don't want to see Kachenka again," poor Kubik said to himself. "Twice I've brought back the best betrothal gift and each time I've got a beating for it. I wonder what they would say if I brought home a frog for a bride! Then they would have something to laugh at!"

So he took a different path through the forest but again he hadn't gone far before the old frog hopped up in front of him. This time Kubik turned and ran. The old frog called after him but the louder she called the faster he ran.

He ran on and on until suddenly a great snake stopped him. The snake reared high its head, then dropped into a coil. Again it reared up and swayed from side to side threatening to strike if Kubik went on. So Kubik saw that fate was determined that he should marry a frog and reluctantly he turned back.

The snake led him to the cliff, where the old frog

greeted him kindly and thanked the snake for his faithful service.

Poor Kubik! He was very tired and very unhappy. When you come to think of it, who wouldn't be unhappy at the prospect of being united for life to a frog?

Kubik was so tired that presently he fell asleep and it was just as well he did, for at least in dreams he could forget his troubles.

The next morning when he woke and rubbed his eyes, he found himself lying on a soft feather bed, white as snow, in a splendid room with decorations that were fit for a king. A fine silken shirt lay spread out on a chair beside the bed and beyond the chair was a stand with a silver basin. When he got up attendants came running in carrying clothes of richly woven cloth of gold. They dressed Kubik and they combed his hair until they had him looking like a young prince. Then they brought him breakfast and there was cream with the coffee and I would have you know that this was only the second time in his life that Kubik had ever had cream with his coffee!

Kubik did not know what to think of it all. His head went round and round. When he looked out the window he saw no trace of cliff or caverns or forest.

Instead he saw a big town with streets and houses and people going to and fro.

Presently music began to play under the window, a great crowd gathered and soon attendants came in to escort Lord Kubik out. As he reached the castle gate, the people cheered and a coach and six drove up. Two ladies were in it, a mother and daughter, both dressed in beautiful silks. They alighted from the coach and when they saw Kubik they smiled and came toward him with outstretched hands.

"You don't know us, do you, Kubik?" the older lady said. "I was that old frog who coaxed you to the cliff and this, my beautiful daughter, was the other little frog, the very ugly one, that you feared you would have to take home to your father's house as your bride. You see, Kubik, we were all under an evil enchantment. Many years ago a wicked magician brought ruin on us and our kingdom. He changed our subjects into snakes and us into frogs and turned our fine city into a rocky cliff. Nothing could break the enchantment until some one should come and ask a betrothal gift from my daughter. We lived in the forest for years and years and all those years I begged all the people who wandered by to help us but they only trod on us or turned away from us in disgust.

You, Kubik, were the first not to scorn us for our ugly looks. By this you broke the evil spell that held us and now we are all free. As a reward you shall marry my daughter, the Princess Kachenka, and be made king!"

Then the old queen took Kubik by the hand and led him to the royal coach, where she made him sit between her and the princess. Music played and the people cheered, and in this style they drove to Kubik's native village and to his father's house.

The old man was in the yard chopping firewood and his older sons were helping him. They, too, had brought home their brides, plain country girls from poor farms, and at that moment they were all awaiting Kubik's arrival.

"Look, father," the oldest son cried, "some fine folk are turning in here!"

"We're not behind in our taxes, are we?" the second son asked.

"Hush!" the old man whispered. "I have nothing to fear. My affairs are all in good order."

He put his cap respectfully under his arm and stood bareheaded and both his sons followed his example.

The coach drove straight into the yard and a handsome young lord and two beautiful ladies alighted.

The handsome young lord greeted the old man and his sons and they bowed and scraped and pressed their hats under their arms tighter and tighter.

Then they all stepped into the old kitchen that was black with the smoke of many years and the handsome young lord sat down on the bench behind the table as though that was where he always sat. The two brothers and their brides shrank back against the oven and held their breath.

Then the handsome young lord said to the old man: "Don't you know me?"

"Where could I ever have seen your lordship?" the farmer asked, humbly. He kept bobbing so low it was a wonder he didn't bump his head against the floor.

"And do neither of your sons know me? I think these are your sons, aren't they?"

The farmer kept on bowing and the two sons looked down, too embarrassed to speak.

At length the handsome young lord said: "What, don't you know your own son, Kubik, whom you used to beat for stealing when he showed you his betrothal gifts?"

At that the old man looked at him closely and cried out: "Bless my soul, I believe it is our Kubik!

Kubik Greeting His Old Father

But who could recognize the boy! . . . And is this his bride? That settles it! Kubik shall have the farm! Kubik has brought home the most beautiful bride!"

"Kubik doesn't need the farm," the old queen said, "nor will you need it any longer nor your other sons. You will all come home with us to our kingdom over which Kubik is now king. And may God grant you many years to live on in peace and quiet."

The farmer was overjoyed at this arrangement. He embraced his son, and his son's bride, and his son's royal mother-in-law.

He gave his farm to the poorest man in the village and then he and his sons accompanied Kubik back to his kingdom. There he lived long in peace and comfort enjoying the thought that good fortune had come to them all on account of his determination not to divide the farm.

The poor man who inherited the farm prayed for him and his sons every night and never tired of telling the story of how Kubik became a king and his brothers courtiers.

So for many years the memory of Kubik was kept green. Now people are beginning to forget him, so I thought it was time that I tell his story again

GRANDFATHER'S EYES

THE STORY OF THREE WICKED YEZINKAS

GRANDFATHER'S EYES

ONCE upon a time there was a poor boy whom everybody called Yanechek. His father and mother were dead and he was forced to start out alone in the world to make a living. For a long time he could find nothing to do. He wandered on and on and at last he came to a little house that stood by itself near the edge of the woods. An old man sat on the doorstep and Yanechek could see that he was blind, for there were empty holes where his eyes used to be.

Some goats that were penned in a shed near the house began bleating and the old man said:

"You poor things, you want to go to pasture, don't you? But I can't see to drive you and I have no one else to send."

"Send me, grandfather," Yanechek said. "Take me as your goatherd and let me work for you."

"Who are you?" the old man asked.

Yanechek told him who he was and the old man agreed to take him.

"And now," he said, "drive the goats to pasture. But one thing, Yanechek: don't take them to the hill over there in the woods or the Yezinkas may get you! That's where they caught me!"

Now Yanechek knew that the Yezinkas were wicked witches who lived in a cave in the woods and went about in the guise of beautiful young women. If they met you they would greet you modestly and say something like "God bless you!" to make you think they were good and kind and then, once they had you in their power, they would put you to sleep and gouge out your eyes! Oh, yes, Yanechek knew about the Yezinkas.

"Never fear, grandfather, the Yezinkas won't get me!"

The first day and the second day Yanechek kept the goats near home. But the third day he said to himself: "I think I'll try the hill in the woods. There's better grass there and I'm not afraid of the Yezinkas."

Before he started out he cut three long slender switches from a blackberry bramble, wound them into small coils, and hid them in the crown of his hat.

Then he drove the goats through the woods where they nibbled at leaves and branches, beside a deep river where they paused to drink, and up the grassy slopes of the hill.

There the goats scattered this way and that and Yanechek sat down on a stone in the shade. He was hardly seated when he looked up and there before him, dressed all in white, stood the most beautiful maiden in the world. Her skin was red as roses and white as milk, her eyes were black as sloe berries, and her hair, dark as the raven's wing, fell about her shoulders in long waving tresses. She smiled and offered Yanechek a big red apple.

" God bless you, shepherd boy," she said. " Here's something for you that grew in my own garden."

But Yanechek knew that she must be a Yezinka and that, if he ate the apple, he would fall asleep and then she would gouge out his eyes. So he said, politely: " No, thank you, beautiful maiden. My master has a tree in his garden with apples that are bigger than yours and I have eaten as many as I want."

When the maiden saw that Yanechek was not to be coaxed, she disappeared.

Presently a second maiden came, more beautiful,

if possible, than the first. In her hand she carried a lovely red rose.

"God bless you, shepherd boy," she said. "Isn't this a lovely rose? I picked it myself from the hedge. How fragrant it is! Will you smell it?"

She offered him the rose but Yanechek refused it.

"No, thank you, beautiful maiden. My master's garden is full of roses much sweeter than yours and I smell roses all the time."

At that the second maiden shrugged her shoulders and disappeared.

Presently a third one came, the youngest and most beautiful of them all. In her hand she carried a golden comb.

"God bless you, shepherd boy."

"Good day to you, beautiful maiden."

She smiled at Yanechek and said: "Truly you are a handsome lad, but you would be handsomer still if your hair were nicely combed. Come, let me comb it for you."

Yanechek said nothing but he took off his hat without letting the maiden see what was hidden in its crown. She came up close to him and then, just as she was about to comb his hair, he whipped out one of the long blackberry switches and struck her over the hands. She screamed and tried to escape but she could not because it is the fate of a Yezinka not to be able to move if ever a human being strikes her over the hands with a switch of bramble.

So Yanechek took her two hands and bound them together with the long thorny switch while she wept and struggled.

"Help, sisters! Help!" she cried.

At that the two other Yezinkas came running and when they saw what had happened they, too, began to weep and to beg Yanechek to unbind their sister's hands and let her go.

But Yanechek only laughed and said: "No. You unbind them."

"But, Yanechek, how can we? Our hands are soft and the thorns will prick us."

However, when they saw that Yanechek was not to be moved, they went to their sister and tried to help her. Whereupon Yanechek whipped out the other two blackberry switches and struck them also on their soft pretty hands, first one and then the other. After that they, too, could not move and it was easy enough to bind them and make them prisoners.

"Now I've got the three of you, you wicked Yezinkas!" Yanechek said. "It was you who gouged out my poor old master's eyes, you know it was! And you shall not escape until you do as I ask."

He left them there and ran home to his master to whom he said: " Come, grandfather, for I have found a means of restoring your eyes!"

He took the old man by the hand and led him through the woods, along the bank of the river, and up the grassy hillside where the three Yezinkas were still struggling and weeping.

Then he said to the first of them: " Tell me now where my master's eyes are. If you don't tell me, I'll throw you into the river."

The first Yezinka pretended she didn't know. So Yanechek lifted her up and started down the hill toward the river.

That frightened the maiden and she cried out: " Don't throw me into the river, Yanechek, and I'll find you your master's eyes, I promise you I will!"

So Yanechek put her down and she led him to a cave in the hillside where she and her wicked sisters had piled up a great heap of eyes—all kinds of eyes they were: big eyes, little eyes, black eyes, red eyes, blue eyes, green eyes—every kind of eye in the world that you can think of.

She went to the heap and picked out two eyes

which she said were the right ones. But when the poor old man tried to look through them, he cried out in fright:

"I see nothing but dark treetops with sleeping birds and flying bats! These are not my eyes! They are owls' eyes! Take them out! Take them out!"

When Yanechek saw how the first Yezinka had deceived him, without another word he picked her up, threw her into the river, and that was the end of her.

Then he said to the second sister: "Now you tell me where my master's eyes are."

At first she, too, pretended she didn't know, but when Yanechek threatened to throw her likewise into the river, she was glad enough to lead him back to the cave and pick out two eyes that she said were the right ones.

But when the poor old man tried to look through them, again he cried out in fright: "I see nothing but tangled underbrush and snapping teeth and hot red tongues! These are not my eyes! They are wolves' eyes! Take them out! Take them out!"

When Yanechek saw how the second Yezinka had deceived him, without another word he picked her up, and threw her also into the river, and that was the end of her.

Then Yanechek said to the third sister: "Now you tell me where my master's eyes are."

At first she, too, pretended she didn't know, but when Yanechek threatened to throw her likewise into the river, she was glad enough to lead him to the cave and pick out two eyes that she said were the right ones.

But when the poor old man tried to look through them, again he cried out in fright: "I see nothing but swirling waters and flashing fins! These are not my eyes! They are fishes' eyes! Take them out! Take them out!"

When Yanechek saw how the third Yezinka had deceived him, without another word he was ready to serve her as he had served her sisters. But she begged him not to drown her and she said:

"Let me try again, Yanechek, and I'll find you the right eyes, I promise you I will!"

So Yanechek let her try again and from the very bottom of the heap she picked out two more eyes that she swore were the right ones.

When the old man looked through them, he clapped his hands and said: "These are my own eyes, praise God! Now I can see as well as ever!"

After that the old man and Yanechek lived on happily together. Yanechek pastured the goats and the old man made cheeses at home and they ate them together. And you may be sure that the third Yezinka never showed herself again on that hill!

RATTLE-RATTLE-RATTLE AND CHINK-CHINK-CHINK

THE STORY OF LONG BEARD, THE DWARF, AND THE TWO SISTERS

RATTLE-RATTLE-RATTLE AND CHINK-CHINK-CHINK

THERE was once a poor man whose wife died leaving him a daughter. The little girl's name was Lenka. She was a good little girl, cheerful and obedient and very industrious, and she did all she could to make her father comfortable.

After some time the man married again. His second wife also had a little girl just Lenka's age. Her name was Dorla. Dorla was a lazy, ill-natured child, always quarreling and bickering. Yet her mother thought Dorla was perfect and she was always praising her to her husband.

" See what a good child my Dorla is," she would say to him. " She works and spins and never says a cross word. Very different from your good-for-nothing Lenka who always breaks everything she touches and does nothing in return for all the good food she eats! "

She never stopped nagging and scolding her poor

stepchild and complaining about her to her husband. Lenka was patient and went on quietly doing what was right, and she was always polite to her stepmother, and kind to her ill-natured stepsister.

She and Dorla used to go to spinning bees together. Dorla would play and waste her time and hardly fill one spindle. Lenka always worked industriously and usually filled two or three spools. Yet, when the two girls got home, the mother always took Dorla's halffilled spindle and said to the father: "See what beautiful yarn my Dorla spins!" She would hide Lenka's spools and say: "Your Lenka did nothing but play and waste her time!"

And before other people she talked the same way, pretending Dorla did everything that she didn't do and saying that good industrious Lenka was lazy and good-for-nothing.

One night when the two girls were walking home together from a spinning bee, they came to a ditch in the road. Dorla jumped quickly across and then reached back her hand and said:

"My dear sister, let me hold your spindle. You may fall and hurt yourself."

Poor Lenka, suspecting nothing unkind, handed Dorla her full spindle. Dorla took it and ran home and then boasted to her mother and her stepfather how much she had spun.

"Lenka," she said, "has no yarn at all. She did nothing but play and waste her time."

"You see," said the woman to her husband. "This is what I'm always telling you but you never believe me. That Lenka of yours is a lazy, good-for-nothing girl who expects me and my poor daughter to do all the work. I'm not going to stand her in the house any longer. Tomorrow morning out she goes to make her own way in the world. Then perhaps she'll understand what a good home she's had with me!"

The poor man tried to defend Lenka but his wife would hear nothing. Lenka must go and that was all there was to it.

Early the next morning while it was still dark the woman started Lenka off. She gave her a sack that she said was full of good meal and smoked meat and bread. But instead of meal she put in ashes, instead of smoked meat straw, and instead of bread stones.

"Here is meal and smoked meat and bread for your journey," she said. "You will be a long time finding any one who will be as good to you as I have been! Now be off with you and never let me see you again! Let your father put you out in service if he can!"

The poor man put his ax on his shoulder and started off with Lenka. He had no place to take her and he hardly knew what to do. He led her off into the mountains, where he built her a little two-room hut. He was ashamed to tell her that he was going to leave her alone, so he said to her:

"You stay here, my dear child, while I go farther into the forest and cut you some firewood."

But instead of cutting her firewood, he hung his mallet on a beech tree and whenever the wind blew, the mallet made a knocking sound. All afternoon poor little Lenka hearing the knock-knock of the mallet thought to herself: "There is my dear father chopping wood for me!"

When evening came and he hadn't returned, Lenka went out to find him, but all she could find was the mallet going knock-knock on the tree. Then the poor girl realized that her father had deceived her but she forgave him, for she knew that it was her stepmother's fault.

She went back to the little hut to get her supper, but when she opened the sack her stepmother had given her, instead of meal and smoked meat and bread, she found only ashes and straw and stones. Then indeed did Lenka feel deserted and sitting down she cried with loneliness and hunger.

While she was crying an old beggar with a long beard came into the hut.

" God grant you happiness, my child," he said.

" May He grant you the same, old father," Lenka said, standing up and bowing politely.

" Thank you, my child, thank you. And now will you be so kind as to wash my face and give me a bite of supper? "

" Indeed, old father, I'd gladly wash your face and give you food, but there's no water here and nothing to carry it in. And as for food, my stepmother filled the sack with ashes, straw, and stones."

" That's nothing, my child. Just go behind the hut and you will find a spring."

Lenka went and there, sure enough, was a clear bubbling spring and on the ground beside it a bucket. She filled the bucket and carried it back to the hut.

As she entered the door she could hardly believe her eyes, for on the wall she saw a row of shining plates, big plates and little plates, and cups, and everything else that ought to be in a kitchen. The old beggar had started a fire, so Lenka at once put on water to boil.

"Look in the sack," the beggar said.

Lenka untied the sack again and here it was full of fine meal and bread and smoked meat!

So now Lenka lost no time in preparing a good supper. Then she washed the old beggar's face and hands and together they ate. After supper Lenka spread out her ragged clothes on the floor of the inner room and put the beggar in there for the night. She herself stretched out on the kitchen bench. It was a hard bed but Lenka made no complaint and presently she fell asleep.

At midnight there was a knocking at the door and a voice called out:

> "*A man am I*
> *Six inches high,*
> *But a long, long beard*
> *Hangs from my chin.*
> *Open the door*
> *And let me in!*"

Lenka jumped down and opened the door and there before her stood a tiny dwarf with a long beard.

He was Long Beard who lived in the mountains and of whom Lenka had often heard stories.

He came in dragging after him a heavy bag of golden ducats.

" I was that old beggar," he said, " whose face you washed and with whom you shared your supper. These ducats are to reward you for your kindness. Now go into your bedroom and lie down comfortably."

As he said this he vanished.

Lenka went into her bedroom and there, instead of her few rags on the floor, was a fine feather bed and coverlets and a painted chest full of clothes. Lenka lay down on the feather bed and instantly fell asleep.

On the third day her father came, supposing by that time Lenka had either died of hunger or been devoured by wild beasts. At least, he thought, he would gather together her bones.

But when he reached the hut he rubbed his eyes in surprise. Instead of the rough hut, there was a pretty little cottage and instead of a handful of bones there was a happy girl singing away at her spinning.

" My daughter, my daughter! " he cried. " How are you? "

" Very well, dear father. You couldn't have found a better place for me."

She told him how happy she was and how pleasantly she passed the time, spinning and singing and working. Then she took a table-cloth and filled it with golden ducats and gave it to him.

So he went away very happy, thanking God for the good fortune that had come to Lenka.

As he neared home, the old dog that lay at the door said to the stepmother:

"Bow-wow, mistress, here comes the master. It's chink-chink the money before him and chink-chink the money behind him!"

"Not so, old dog!" the stepmother cried. "It's rattle-rattle bones before him and rattle-rattle bones behind him!"

Now when the man came into the cottage, he said: "Wife, give me a basket and let me empty this table-cloth."

"What!" she cried. "Do you expect me to give you a basket for your daughter's bones?"

But he began to chink the golden ducats and then she got a basket fast enough.

When she had all the ducats safely put away she said:

"Isn't it just like you to find a place like that for your Lenka! But what have you ever done for my poor Dorla? Tomorrow you will take her out into the world and find a good place for her!"

So she got ready for Dorla a fine new bed and stylish clothes and as much good food as she could carry. The next day the man took Dorla out into the mountains and built her a little hut of two rooms.

Dorla sat in the hut and thought about the good supper she was going to cook for herself.

In the evening the same old beggar came and said to her:

"May God grant you happiness, my child. Won't you please wash my face?"

"Wash your face, indeed!" cried Dorla in a rage. "This is what I'll do to you!" And she took a stick and drove the old beggar away.

"Very well!" he muttered. "Very well! Very well!"

Then Dorla cooked herself a fine supper. After she had eaten every bite of it herself, she lay down on the bed and went soundly to sleep.

At midnight Long Beard knocked at the door and called out:

> "*A man am I*
> *Six inches high,*

But a long, long beard
Hangs from my chin.
Open the door
And let me in!"

Then Dorla was very frightened and she hid in the corner. Long Beard broke open the door and he caught Dorla and he shook her out of her skin. It served her right, too, for she was a wicked, spiteful girl and she had never been kind to anybody in her life.

Long Beard left her bones in a heap on the floor, and he hung her skin on the nail at the back of the door. Then he put her grinning skull in the window.

On the third day Dorla's mother gave her husband a brand new table-cloth and said:

"Go now and see how my Dorla is getting on. Here is a table-cloth for the ducats."

So the man took the table-cloth and went to the mountains. As he came near the hut, he saw something in the window that looked like grinning teeth. He said to himself:

"Dorla must be very happy to be smiling at me from this distance."

But when he reached the hut all he found of Dorla

was a heap of bones on the floor, the skin hanging on the nail behind the door, and the skull grinning in the window.

Without a word he gathered the bones into the table-cloth and started back.

As he neared home the old dog said:

" Bow-wow, mistress, here comes the master and it's rattle-rattle before him and rattle-rattle behind him."

" Not so, old dog! " cried the woman. " It's chink-chink before him, and chink-chink behind him! "

But the old dog kept on barking and saying:

" No, no, bow-wow, it's rattle-rattle before him and rattle-rattle behind him! "

In a rage the woman took a stick and beat the dog.

Then the man stepped into the cottage and at once his wife brought out a basket for the ducats. But when he shook out the table-cloth there was only the rattle-rattle of bones.

THE BIRD WITH THE GOLDEN GIZZARD

THE STORY OF TWO BROTHERS

THE BIRD WITH THE GOLDEN GIZZARD

THERE was once a poor man who had a large family. He was so poor that he had nothing to feed the children. For three days they had had no food. On the third day as the father was out cutting osiers he saw, sitting in a bush, a small bird that shone like gold.

" If I could snare that bird," he thought to himself, " and take it home, the children would be amused and perhaps forget they were hungry."

So he caught the bird and carried it home and, sure enough, the children were so delighted that for two days they didn't cry for food.

On the third day the bird laid a golden egg. The oldest boy took the egg to the goldsmith to sell it. The goldsmith examined it and said:

" I don't believe I have money enough to buy this egg."

" Just give me some bread," the boy said. " That will be enough."

The goldsmith gave him two loaves of bread, one under each arm, and filled his pockets with golden ducats. So for once the whole family had all it could eat and still there was money left over.

Two days later the bird laid another golden egg which the boy carried to the goldsmith and sold for the same price.

Now the goldsmith had a son who said he would like to see this wonderful bird. So he went home with the boy. He looked the bird over very carefully and under its wings he discovered an inscription that no one else had seen. The inscription read:

Whoever eats my heart will become king.

Whoever eats my gizzard will find under his head each morning a heap of golden ducats.

The youth went home and told his father about the strange inscription. They talked the matter over and at last decided that it would be well for the young man to marry the poor man's oldest daughter provided he could get the golden bird as dowry.

The goldsmith went to see the girl's father and after some discussion the marriage was arranged.

The wedding day arrived. The bridegroom ordered

the bird to be roasted and ready to be put on the table when the bridal party came home from church. It was his intention to eat the heart himself and have his bride eat the gizzard.

The children of the family cried bitterly at the thought of losing their pretty bird, but the bridegroom, of course, had his way.

Now two of the boys stayed home from the wedding and they decided that they would like very much to taste the roast bird if only they could find a piece that nobody would miss. They did not dare take a leg or a wing, but they thought it would be safe to pick out a morsel from the inside. So one boy ate the heart, the other the gizzard. Then they were so frightened at what they had done that they ran away and never came back.

When the bride and groom returned from church, the bird was carried to the table. The groom looked at once for the heart and the gizzard and was greatly shocked at their disappearance.

The two boys who had gone out into the world found work with a merchant. They slept together and every morning the merchant's wife found a heap of golden ducats under the feather bed. She didn't know to which boy they belonged. She took them and saved them for a whole year until they filled a hogshead.

At the end of a year the boys decided to go out again into the world. The merchant showed them all the ducats his wife had found in their bed and he said to them:

"Take with you as many as you want now and when you come back you may have the rest."

The brothers parted company and each set out alone, the one to the left, the other to the right.

The younger brother came to a tavern. The landlady had two daughters who were so sharp at cards that they very soon won all the money he had. When he was picked clean he asked them to stop playing until the next morning when he would again have plenty of money.

Sure enough in the morning when he got up he had all the money he wanted. The girls asked him where it came from and he told them.

When they heard about the gizzard he had swallowed, they put something in his wine that made him sick at his stomach and he threw up the gizzard. The younger girl instantly snatched it, washed it, and swallowed it herself. Then as he had no more money they drove the poor boy away.

As he wandered in the fields he grew very hungry. He came to a meadow where he found a kind of sorrel that he ate. As soon as he ate it he turned into a goat and went jumping about the bushes nibbling at the leaves. He chanced to eat a kind of leaf that changed him back into himself.

" Ah," he thought, " now I know what to do! "

He picked some of the sorrel and some of the other leaves and went straight back to the tavern. He told them there that he was bringing them a present of a new kind of spinach that tasted very good. They asked him would he cook it for them.

The cook tasted it and at once she turned into a goat. The serving maid came into the kitchen and when she saw a goat there she drove it out. The youth asked the maid would she like to taste the new spinach. She tasted it and immediately she turned into a goat. Then when the landlady and her two daughters tasted it they, too, turned into goats.

He fed the cook and the serving maid some of the other leaves and they turned back into themselves. But the other three he left as goats.

He made halters for them and then he hitched them up and drove off.

He drove on and on until he came to a town where

the king was building himself a castle. Now this king was his brother who had eaten the magic bird's heart. The king's workmen were hauling stone for the new castle, so he decided to put his goats to work hauling stone. He loaded his cart heavier than all the other carts.

The king noticed him and recognized him and asked him where he got those goats. So he told the king the whole story. The king thought the goats had been punished long enough and begged his brother to have pity on them and restore them. He took the king's advice and did so.

When they were once more human beings, he married the girl who had swallowed the gizzard. They soon became very rich, for every morning there was a heap of golden ducats under her head.

THE WOOD MAIDEN

THE STORY OF BETUSHKA AND
THE GOLDEN BIRCH LEAVES

THE WOOD MAIDEN

BETUSHKA was a little girl. Her mother was a poor widow with nothing but a tumble-down cottage and two little nanny-goats. But poor as they were Betushka was always cheerful. From spring till autumn she pastured the goats in the birch wood. Every morning when she left home her mother gave her a little basket with a slice of bread and a spindle.

"See that you bring home a full spindle," her mother always said.

Betushka had no distaff, so she wound the flax around her head. Then she took the little basket and went romping and singing behind the goats to the birch wood. When they got there she sat down under a tree and pulled the fibers of the flax from her head with her left hand, and with her right hand let down the spindle so that it went humming along the ground. All the while she sang until the woods echoed and the little goats nibbled away at the leaves and grass.

When the sun showed midday, she put the spindle

aside, called the goats and gave them a mouthful of bread so that they wouldn't stray, and ran off into the woods to hunt berries or any other wild fruit that was in season. Then when she had finished her bread and fruit, she jumped up, folded her arms, and danced and sang.

The sun smiled at her through the green of the trees and the little goats, resting on the grass, thought: "What a merry little shepherdess we have!"

After her dance she went back to her spinning and worked industriously. In the evening when she got home her mother never had to scold her because the spindle was empty.

One day at noon just after she had eaten and, as usual, was going to dance, there suddenly stood before her a most beautiful maiden. She was dressed in white gauze that was fine as a spider's web. Long golden hair fell down to her waist and on her head she wore a wreath of woodland flowers.

Betushka was speechless with surprise and alarm.

The maiden smiled at her and said in a sweet voice:

"Betushka, do you like to dance?"

Her manner was so gracious that Betushka no longer felt afraid, and answered:

" Oh, I could dance all day long! "

" Come, then, let us dance together," said the maiden. " I'll teach you."

With that she tucked up her skirt, put her arm about Betushka's waist, and they began to dance. At once such enchanting music sounded over their heads that Betushka's heart went one-two with the dancing. The musicians sat on the branches of the birch trees. They were clad in little frock coats, black and gray and many-colored. It was a carefully chosen orchestra that had gathered at the bidding of the beautiful maiden: larks, nightingales, finches, linnets, thrushes, blackbirds, and showy mocking-birds.

Betushka's cheeks burned, her eyes shone. She forgot her spinning, she forgot her goats. All she could do was gaze at her partner who was moving with such grace and lightness that the grass didn't seem to bend under her slender feet.

They danced from noon till sundown and yet Betushka wasn't the least bit tired. Then they stopped dancing, the music ceased, and the maiden disappeared as suddenly as she had come.

Betushka looked around. The sun was sinking behind the wood. She put her hands to the unspun flax on her head and remembered the spindle that was lying unfilled on the grass. She took down the flax and laid it with the spindle in the little basket. Then she called the goats and started home.

She reproached herself bitterly that she had allowed the beautiful maiden to beguile her and she told herself that another time she would not listen to her. She was so quiet that the little goats, missing her merry song, looked around to see whether it was really their own little shepherdess who was following them. Her mother, too, wondered why she didn't sing and questioned her.

" Are you sick, Betushka? "

" No, dear mother, I'm not sick, but I've been singing too much and my throat is dry."

She knew that her mother did not reel the yarn at once, so she hid the spindle and the unspun flax, hoping to make up tomorrow what she had not done today. She did not tell her mother one word about the beautiful maiden.

The next day she felt cheerful again and as she drove the goats to pasture she sang merrily. At the birch wood she sat down to her spinning, singing all the while, for with a song on the lips work falls from the hands more easily.

Noonday came. Betushka gave a bit of bread to

each of the goats and ran off to the woods for her berries. Then she ate her luncheon.

"Ah, my little goats," she sighed, as she brushed up the crumbs for the birds, "I mustn't dance today."

"Why mustn't you dance today?" a sweet voice asked, and there stood the beautiful maiden as though she had fallen from the clouds.

Betushka was worse frightened than before and she closed her eyes tight. When the maiden repeated her question, Betushka answered timidly:

"Forgive me, beautiful lady, for not dancing with you. If I dance with you I cannot spin my stint and then my mother will scold me. Today before the sun sets I must make up for what I lost yesterday."

"Come, child, and dance," the maiden said. "Before the sun sets we'll find some way of getting that spinning done!"

She tucked up her skirt, put her arm about Betushka, the musicians in the treetops struck up, and off they whirled. The maiden danced more beautifully than ever. Betushka couldn't take her eyes from her. She forgot her goats, she forgot her spinning. All she wanted to do was to dance on forever.

At sundown the maiden paused and the music stopped. Then Betushka, clasping her hands to her head, where the unspun flax was twined, burst into tears. The beautiful maiden took the flax from her head, wound it round the stem of a slender birch, grasped the spindle, and began to spin. The spindle hummed along the ground and filled in no time. Before the sun sank behind the woods all the flax was spun, even that which was left over from the day before. The maiden handed Betushka the full spindle and said:

" Remember my words:

> *Reel and grumble not!*
> *Reel and grumble not!* "

When she said this, she vanished as if the earth had swallowed her.

Betushka was very happy now and she thought to herself on her way home: " Since she is so good and kind, I'll dance with her again if she asks me. Oh, how I hope she does! "

She sang her merry little song as usual and the goats trotted cheerfully along.

She found her mother vexed with her, for she had wanted to reel yesterday's yarn and had discovered that the spindle was not full.

"What were you doing yesterday," she scolded, "that you didn't spin your stint?"

Betushka hung her head. "Forgive me, mother. I danced too long." Then she showed her mother today's spindle and said: "See, today I more than made up for yesterday."

Her mother said no more but went to milk the goats and Betushka put away the spindle. She wanted to tell her mother her adventure, but she thought to herself: "No, I'll wait. If the beautiful lady comes again, I'll ask her who she is and then I'll tell mother." So she said nothing.

On the third morning she drove the goats as usual to the birch wood. The goats went to pasture and Betushka, sitting down under a tree, began to spin and sing. When the sun pointed to noon, she laid her spindle on the grass, gave the goats a mouthful of bread, gathered some strawberries, ate her luncheon, and then, giving the crumbs to the birds, she said cheerily:

"Today, my little goats, I will dance for you!"

She jumped up, folded her arms, and was about to see whether she could move as gracefully as the beautiful maiden, when the maiden herself stood before her.

"Let us dance together," she said. She smiled at Betushka, put her arm about her, and as the music above their heads began to play, they whirled round and round with flying feet. Again Betushka forgot the spindle and the goats. Again she saw nothing but the beautiful maiden whose body was lithe as a willow shoot. Again she heard nothing but the enchanting music to which her feet danced of themselves.

They danced from noon till sundown. Then the maiden paused and the music ceased. Betushka looked around. The sun was already set behind the woods. She clasped her hands to her head and looking down at the unfilled spindle she burst into tears.

"Oh, what will my mother say?" she cried.

"Give me your little basket," the maiden said, "and I will put something in it that will more than make up for today's stint."

Betushka handed her the basket and the maiden took it and vanished. In a moment she was back. She returned the basket and said:

" Look not inside until you're home!
Look not inside until you're home!"

As she said these words she was gone as if a wind had blown her away.

Betushka wanted awfully to peep inside but she was afraid to. The basket was so light that she wondered whether there was anything at all in it. Was the lovely lady only fooling her? Halfway home she peeped in to see.

Imagine her feelings when she found the basket was full of birch leaves! Then indeed did Betushka burst into tears and reproach herself for being so simple. In her vexation she threw out a handful of leaves and was going to empty the basket when she thought to herself:

" No, I'll keep what's left as litter for the goats."

She was almost afraid to go home. She was so quiet that again the little goats wondered what ailed their shepherdess.

Her mother was waiting for her in great excitement.

" For heaven's sake, Betushka, what kind of a spool did you bring home yesterday? "

" Why? " Betushka faltered.

" When you went away this morning I started to reel that yarn. I reeled and reeled and the spool remained full. One skein, two skeins, three skeins, and still the spool was full. 'What evil spirit has spun that?' I cried out impatiently, and instantly the yarn disappeared from the spindle as if blown away. Tell me, what does it mean? "

So Betushka confessed and told her mother all she knew about the beautiful maiden.

" Oh," cried her mother in amazement, " that was a wood maiden! At noon and midnight the wood maidens dance. It is well you are not a little boy or she might have danced you to death! But they are often kind to little girls and sometimes make them rich presents. Why didn't you tell me? If I hadn't grumbled, I could have had yarn enough to fill the house! "

Betushka thought of the little basket and wondered if there might be something under the leaves. She took out the spindle and unspun flax and looked in once more.

" Mother! " she cried. " Come here and see! "

Her mother looked and clapped her hands. The birch leaves were all turned to gold!

Betushka reproached herself bitterly: " She told me not to look inside until I got home, but I didn't obey."

" It's lucky you didn't empty the whole basket," her mother said.

The next morning she herself went to look for the

handful of leaves that Betushka had thrown away. She found them still lying in the road but they were only birch leaves.

But the riches which Betushka brought home were enough. Her mother bought a farm with fields and cattle. Betushka had pretty clothes and no longer had to pasture goats.

But no matter what she did, no matter how cheerful and happy she was, still nothing ever again gave her quite so much pleasure as the dance with the wood maiden. She often went to the birch wood in the hope of seeing the maiden again. But she never did.

THE GOLDEN SPINNING WHEEL

THE STORY OF KING DOBROMIL AND THE GOOD DOBRUNKA

Alike in Feature but Utterly Different in Disposition

THE GOLDEN SPINNING WHEEL

THERE was once a poor woman who had twin daughters. The girls were exactly alike in face and feature but utterly different in disposition. Dobrunka was kind, industrious, obedient, and everything a good girl ought to be. Zloboha, her sister, was spiteful, disobedient, lazy, and proud. In fact, she had just about as many faults as a person could have. Yet strange to say the mother loved Zloboha much better and made everything easy for her.

They lived in a cottage a few miles from town. The cottage stood by itself in a little clearing in the woods. Hardly any one ever passed it except occasionally some man who had lost his way in the woods.

The mother put her favorite, Zloboha, out to service so that she might learn city ways, but she kept Dobrunka at home to do the housework and take care of the garden. Dobrunka always began the day by feeding the goats, then she prepared the breakfast, swept the kitchen, and when everything else was done she sat down at her spinning wheel and spun.

She seldom benefited from the yarn she spun so carefully, for her mother always sold it in town and spent the money on clothes for Zloboha. Yet Dobrunka loved her mother although she never had a kind word or a kind look from her the whole day long. She always obeyed her mother instantly and without a frown and no one ever heard her complain about all the work she had to do.

One day when her mother was going to town Dobrunka went part of the way with her, carrying her yarn wrapped up in a kerchief.

"Now see that you're not lazy while I'm away," her mother said, crossly.

"You know, mother, you never have to nag at me. Today when I finish the housework, I'll spin so industriously that you'll be more than satisfied when you get home."

She handed her yarn to her mother and went back to the cottage. Then when she had put the kitchen in order, she sat down to her wheel and began to spin. Dobrunka had a pretty voice, as pretty as any of the song-birds in the forest, and always when she was alone she sang. So today as she sat spinning she sang all the songs she knew, one after the other.

Suddenly she heard outside the trample of a horse.

"Some one is coming," she thought to herself, "some-one who has lost his way in the woods. I'll go see."

She got up from her wheel and peeped out through the small window. A young man was just dismounting from a spirited horse.

"Oh," thought Dobrunka to herself, "what a handsome young lord he is! How well his leather coat fits him! How well his cap with its white feather looks on his black hair! Ah, he is tying his horse and is coming in. I must slip back to my spinning."

The next moment the young man opened the door and stepped into the kitchen. All this happened a long time ago, you see, when there were no locks or bars on the doors, and there didn't have to be because nothing was ever stolen.

"Good day to you, my girl," the young man said to Dobrunka.

"Good day, sir," Dobrunka answered. "What is it, sir, you want?"

"Will you please get me a little water. I'm very thirsty."

"Certainly," Dobrunka said. "Won't you sit down while I'm getting it?"

She ran off, got the pitcher, rinsed it out, and drew some fresh water from the well.

"I wish I could give you something better, sir."

"Nothing could taste better than this," he said, handing her back the empty pitcher. "See, I have taken it all."

Dobrunka put the pitcher away and the young man, while her back was turned, slipped a leather bag, full of money, into the bed.

"I thank you for the drink," he said, as he rose to go. "I'll come again tomorrow if you'll let me."

"Come if you want to," Dobrunka said, modestly.

He took her hand, held it a moment, then leaped upon his horse and galloped off.

Dobrunka sat down again to her wheel and tried to work, but her mind wandered. The image of the young man kept rising before her eyes and I have to confess that, for an expert spinner, she broke her thread pretty often.

Her mother came home in the evening full of praises of Zloboha, who, she said, was growing prettier day by day. Everybody in town admired her and she was fast learning city ways and city manners. It was Zloboha this and Zloboha that for hours.

Finally the old woman remarked: "They say there was a great hunting party out today. Did you hear anything of it?"

"Oh, yes," Dobrunka said. "I forgot to tell you that a young huntsman stopped here to ask for a drink. He was handsomely dressed in leather. You know once when I was in town with you we saw a whole company of men in leather coats with white feathers in their caps. No doubt this young man belonged to the hunting party. When he had his drink, he jumped on his horse and rode off."

Dobrunka forgot to mention that he had taken her hand in parting and promised to come back next day.

When Dobrunka was preparing the bed for the night, the bag of money fell out. In great surprise she picked it up and handed it to her mother.

The old woman looked at her sharply.

"Dobrunka, who gave you all this money?"

"Nobody gave it to me, mother. Perhaps the huntsman slipped it into the bed. I don't know where else it could have come from."

The old woman emptied the bag on the table. They were all gold pieces.

"Good heavens, so much!" she murmured in amazement. "He must be a very rich young lord! Perhaps he saw how poor we were and thought to do a kind deed. May God grant him happiness!"

She gathered the money together and hid it in the chest.

Usually when Dobrunka went to bed after her day's work she fell asleep at once, but tonight she lay awake thinking of the handsome young rider. When she did at last fall asleep it was to dream of him. He was a powerful young lord, it seemed to her, in her dream. He lived in a great palace and she, Dobrunka, was his wife. She thought that they were giving a fine banquet to which all the nobles in the land had been invited. She and her husband arose from the table and went together into another room. He was about to put his arms about her and embrace her when suddenly a black cat sprang between them and buried its claws in Dobrunka's breast. Her heart's blood spurted out and stained her white dress. She cried out in fright and pain and the cry awoke her.

" What a strange dream," she thought to herself. " I wonder what it means. It began so beautifully but the cruel cat spoiled it all. I fear it bodes something ill."

In the morning when she got up, she was still thinking of it.

On other mornings it didn't take Dobrunka long

to dress but this morning she was very slow. She shook out her fresh skirt again and again. She had the greatest trouble in putting on her bodice just right. She spent much time on her hair, into which she plaited the red ribbon that she usually kept for holidays. When at last she was dressed and ready to go about her household duties she looked very fresh and sweet.

As midday came, she found it hard to sit still at her wheel, but kept jumping up on any pretext whatever to run outdoors a moment to see if the young horseman was in sight.

At last she did see him at a distance and, oh, how she hurried back to her stool so that he would never think that she was watching for him.

He rode into the yard, tied his horse, and came into the cottage.

" Good day, Dobrunka," he said, speaking very gently and very respectfully.

Dobrunka's heart was beating so fast that she feared it would jump out of her body. Her mother was in the woods gathering fagots, so she was again alone with him. She managed to return his greeting and to ask him to sit down. Then she went back to her spinning.

The young man came over to her and took her hand.

" How did you sleep, Dobrunka? "

" Very well, sir."

" Did you dream? "

" Yes, I had a very strange dream."

" Tell me about it. I can explain dreams very well."

" But I can't tell this dream to you," Dobrunka said.

" Why not? "

" Because it's about you."

" That's the very reason you ought to tell me," the young man said.

He urged her and begged her until at last Dobrunka did tell him the dream.

" Well now," he said, " that dream of yours except the part about the cat can be realized easily enough."

Dobrunka laughed. " How could I ever become a fine lady? "

" By marrying me," the young man said.

Dobrunka blushed. " Now, sir, you are joking."

" No, Dobrunka, this is no joke. I really mean it. I came back this morning to ask you to marry me. Will you? "

Dobrunka was too surprised to speak, but when the young man took her hand she did not withdraw it.

Just then the old woman came in. The young man greeted her and without any delay declared his intentions. He said he loved Dobrunka and wished to make her his wife and that all he and Dobrunka were waiting for was the mother's consent.

" I have my own house," he added, " and am well able to take care of a wife. And for you too, dear mother, there will always be room in my house and at my table."

The old woman listened to all he had to say and then very promptly gave her blessing.

" Then, my dear one," the young man said to Dobrunka, " go back to your spinning and when you have spun enough for your wedding shift, I shall come for you."

He kissed her, gave his hand to her mother, and, springing on his horse, rode away.

From that time the old woman treated Dobrunka more kindly. She even went so far as to spend on Dobrunka a little of the money the young man had given them, but most of it, of course, went for clothes for Zloboha.

But in those happy days Dobrunka wasn't worrying about anything as unimportant as money. She sat at her wheel and spun away thinking all the while of her fine young lover. Time sped quickly and before she knew it she had spun enough for her wedding shift.

The very day she was finished her lover came. She heard the trample of his horse and ran out to meet him.

" Have you spun enough for your wedding shift? " he asked her as he took her to his heart.

" Yes," Dobrunka said, " I have."

" Then you can ride away with me this moment."

" This moment! " Dobrunka gasped. " Why so quickly? "

" It has to be, my dear one. Tomorrow I go off to war and want you to take my place at home. Then when I come back you'll be there to greet me as my wife."

" But what will my mother say to this? "

" She will have to consent."

They went into the cottage and spoke to the old woman. She was far from pleased with this arrangement, for she had worked out a very different plan in her mind. But what could she do? A rich young bridegroom always has his own way. So she hid her disappointment with a false smile and gave them her blessing.

Then the young man said to her: "Get your things together, mother, and follow Dobrunka, for I don't want her to be lonely while I'm gone. When you get to the city, go to the palace and ask for Dobromil. The people there will tell you where to go."

Dobrunka with tears streaming down her cheeks bid her mother good-by. Dobromil lifted her to the saddle in front of him and away they went like the wind.

The town was in great excitement. There was much hurrying to and fro as the troops were being put in readiness for the morrow. A crowd had gathered at the palace gates and as a young man came galloping up, holding in front of him a lady lovely as the day, the shout went up:

"Here he is! Here he is!"

The people in the courtyard took up the cry and as Dobromil rode through the gate all of them with one voice shouted out:

"Long live our beautiful queen! Long live our noble king!"

Dobrunka was struck with amazement.

"Are you really the king, Dobromil?" she asked, looking into his proud and happy face.

"Yes," he said. "Aren't you glad that I am?"

"I love you," Dobrunka said, "and so whatever you are makes no difference to me. But why did you deceive me?"

"I did not deceive you. I told you that your dream would be realized if you took me for your husband."

In those early times marriage was a simple affair. When a man and woman loved each other and their parents consented to their union, they were looked upon as married. So Dobromil now was able to present Dobrunka to his people as his wife.

There was great rejoicing, music played, and there was feasting and drinking in the banquet hall until dawn. The next day the young husband kissed his lovely bride farewell and rode off to war.

Left alone the young queen strayed through the magnificent palace like a lost lamb. She would have felt more at home rambling through the woods and awaiting the return of her husband in a little cottage than here where she was a lonely stranger. Yet she was not a stranger long, for within half a day she had won every heart by her sweetness and goodness.

The next day she sent for her mother and the old woman soon arrived bringing with her Dobrunka's spinning wheel. So now there was no more excuse for loneliness.

Dobrunka supposed that her mother would be made very happy to find what good fortune had befallen her daughter. The old woman pretended she was, but in her heart she was furious that a king had married Dobrunka and not Zloboha.

After a few days she said, very artfully, to Dobrunka: "I know, my dear daughter, that you think your sister, Zloboha, was not always kind to you in times past. She's sorry now and I want you to forgive her and invite her here to the palace."

"I should have asked her before this," said Dobrunka, "but I didn't suppose she wanted to come. If you wish it, we'll go for her at once."

"Yes, dear daughter, I do wish it."

So the queen ordered the carriage and off they went to fetch Zloboha. When they came to the edge of the woods they alighted and ordered the coachman to await them there. They went on afoot to the cottage where Zloboha was expecting them.

Zloboha came running out to meet them. She threw her arms about her sister's neck and kissed her and wished her happiness. Then the wicked sister and the wicked mother led poor unsuspecting Dobrunka into the house. Once inside Zloboha took a knife that she had ready and struck Dobrunka. Then they cut off Dobrunka's hands and feet, gouged out her eyes, and hid her poor mutilated body in the woods. Zloboha and her mother wrapped up the hands and the feet and the eyes to carry them back with them to the palace because they believed that it would be easier for them to deceive the king if they had with them something that had belonged to Dobrunka.

Then Zloboha put on Dobrunka's clothes and she and her mother rode back to town in the carriage and nobody could tell that she wasn't Dobrunka. In the palace the attendants soon whispered to each other that their mistress was kinder to them at first, but they suspected nothing.

In the meantime poor Dobrunka, who was not quite dead, had been found by a hermit and carried by him to a cave. She awoke to feel a kind hand soothing her wounds and putting some reviving drops between her lips. Of course, she could not see who it was, for she had no eyes. As she regained consciousness she remembered what had happened and began bitterly to upbraid her unnatural mother and her cruel sister.

"Be quiet. Do not complain," a low voice said. "All will yet be well."

"How can all be well," wept poor Dobrunka, "when I have no eyes and no feet and no hands? I shall never again see the bright sun and the green woods. I shall never again hold in my arms my beloved Dobromil. Nor shall I be able to spin fine flax for his shirts! Oh, what did I ever do to you, wicked mother, or to you, cruel sister, that you have done this to me?"

The hermit went to the entrance of the cave and called three times. Soon a boy came running in answer to the call.

"Wait here till I come back," the hermit said.

He returned in a short time with a golden spinning wheel in his arms. He said to the boy:

"My son, take this spinning wheel to town to the king's palace. Sit down in the courtyard near the gate and if any one asks you for how much you will sell the wheel, say: 'For two eyes.' Unless you are offered two eyes for it bring it back."

The boy took the spinning wheel and carried it to town as the hermit directed. He went to the palace and sat down in the courtyard near the gate, just as Zloboha and her mother were returning from a walk.

"Look, mother!" Zloboha cried. "What a gorgeous spinning wheel! I could spin on that myself! Wait. I'll ask whether it's for sale."

She went over to the boy and asked him would he sell the spinning wheel.

"Yes," he said, "if I get what I want."

"What do you want?"

"I want two eyes."

"Two eyes?"

"Yes, two eyes. My father told me to accept nothing for it but two eyes. So I can't sell it for money."

The longer Zloboha looked at the spinning wheel the more beautiful it seemed to her and the more she wanted it. Suddenly she remembered Dobrunka's eyes that she had hidden away.

"Mother," she said, "as a queen I ought to have something no one else has. When the king comes home he will want me to spin, and just think how lovely I should look sitting at this golden wheel. Now we've got those eyes of Dobrunka's. Let us exchange them for the golden spinning wheel. We'll still have the hands and feet."

The mother, who was as foolish as the daughter, agreed. So Zloboha got the eyes and gave them to the boy for the spinning wheel.

The boy hurried back to the forest and handed the eyes to the hermit. The old man took them and gently put them into place. Instantly Dobrunka could see.

The first thing she saw was the old hermit himself with his tall spare figure and long white beard. The last rays of the setting sun shone through the opening of the cave and lighted up his grave and gentle face. He looked to Dobrunka like one of God's own saints.

" How can I ever repay you? " she said, " for all your loving kindness? Oh, that I could cover your hands with kisses! "

" Be quiet, my child," the old man said. " If you are patient all will yet be well."

He went out and soon returned with some delicious fruit on a wooden plate. This he carried over to the bed of leaves and moss upon which Dobrunka was lying and with his own hands he fed Dobrunka as a mother would feed her helpless child. Then he gave her a drink from a wooden cup.

Early the next morning the hermit again called

three times and the boy came running at once. This time the hermit handed him a golden distaff and said:

"Take this distaff and go to the palace. Sit down in the courtyard near the gate. If any one asks you what you want for the distaff, say two feet and don't exchange it for anything else."

Zloboha was standing at a window of the palace looking down into the courtyard when she saw the boy with a golden distaff.

"Mother!" she cried. "Come and see! There's that boy again sitting near the gate and this time he has a golden distaff!"

Mother and daughter at once went out to question the boy.

"What do you want for the distaff?" Zloboha asked.

"Two feet," the boy said.

"Two feet?"

"Yes, two feet."

"Tell me, what will your father do with two feet?"

"I don't know. I never ask my father what he does with anything. But whatever he tells me to do, I do. That is why I can't exchange the distaff for anything but two feet."

"Listen, mother," Zloboha said, "now that I have

a golden spinning wheel, I ought to have a golden distaff to go with it. You know we have those two feet of Dobrunka's hidden away. What if I gave them to the boy? We shall still have Dobrunka's hands."

"Well, do as you please," the old woman said.

So Zloboha went and got Dobrunka's feet, wrapped them up, and gave them to the boy in exchange for the distaff. Delighted with her bargain, Zloboha went to her chamber and the boy hurried back to the forest.

He gave the feet to the hermit and the old man carried them at once inside the cave. Then he rubbed Dobrunka's wounds with some healing salve and stuck on the feet. Dobrunka wanted to jump up from the couch and walk but the old man restrained her.

"Lie quiet where you are until you are all well and then I'll let you get up."

Dobrunka knew that whatever the old hermit said was for her good, so she rested as he ordered.

On the third morning the hermit called the boy and gave him a golden spindle.

"Go to the palace again," he said, "and today offer this spindle for sale. If any one asks you what you want for the spindle, say two hands. Don't accept anything else."

The boy took the golden spindle and when he

reached the palace and sat down in the courtyard near the gate, Zloboha ran up to him at once.

" What do you want for that spindle? " she asked.

" Two hands," the boy said.

" It's a strange thing you won't sell anything for money."

" I have to ask what my father tells me to ask."

Zloboha was in a quandary. She wanted the golden spindle, for it was very beautiful. It would go well with the spinning wheel and would be something to be proud of. Yet she didn't want to be left without anything that had belonged to Dobrunka.

" But really, mother," she whined, " I don't see why I have to keep something of Dobrunka's so that Dobromil will love me as he loved her. I'm sure I'm as pretty as Dobrunka ever was."

" Well," said the old woman, " it would be better if you kept them. I've often heard that's a good way to guard a man's love. However, do as you like."

For a moment Zloboha was undecided. Then, tossing her head, she ran and got the hands and gave them to the boy.

Zloboha took the spindle and, delighted with her bargain, carried it into her chamber where she had the wheel and distaff. The old woman was a little troubled, for she feared Zloboha had acted foolishly. But Zloboha, confident of her beauty and her ability to charm the king, only laughed at her.

As soon as the boy had delivered the hands to the hermit, the old man carried them into the cave. Then he anointed the wounds on Dobrunka's arms with the same healing salve that he used before, and stuck on the hands.

As soon as Dobrunka could move them she jumped up from the couch and, falling at the hermit's feet, she kissed the hands that had been so good to her.

" A thousand thanks to you, my benefactor! " she cried with tears of joy in her eyes. " I can never repay you, I know that, but ask of me anything I can do and I'll do it."

" I ask nothing," the old man said, gently raising her to her feet. " What I did for you I would do for any one. I only did my duty. So say no more about it. And now, my child, farewell. You are to stay here until some one comes for you. Have no concern for food. I shall send you what you need."

Dobrunka wanted to say something to him, but he disappeared and she never saw him again.

Now she was able to run out of the cave and look once more upon God's green world. Now for the first time in her life she knew what it meant to be strong and well. She threw herself on the ground and kissed it. She hugged the slender birches and danced around them, simply bursting with love for every living thing. She reached out longing hands towards the town and would probably have gone there running all the distance but she remembered the words of the old hermit and knew that she must stay where she was.

Meanwhile strange things were happening at the palace. Messengers brought word that the king was returning from war and there was great rejoicing on every side. The king's own household was particularly happy, for service under the new mistress was growing more unpleasant every day. As for Zloboha and her mother, it must be confessed that they were a little frightened over the outcome of their plot.

Finally the king arrived. Zloboha with smiling face went to meet him. He took her to his heart with great tenderness and from that moment Zloboha had no fear that he would recognize her.

A great feast was at once prepared, for the king had brought home with him many of his nobles to rest and make merry after the hardships of war.

Zloboha as she sat at Dobromil's side could not take her eyes off him. The handsome young soldier caught her fancy and she was rejoiced that she had put Dobrunka out of the way.

When they finished feasting, Dobromil asked her: "What have you been doing all this time, my dear Dobrunka? I'm sure you've been spinning."

"That's true, my dear husband," Zloboha said in a flattering tone. "My old spinning wheel got broken, so I bought a new one, a lovely golden one."

"You must show me it at once," the king said, and he took Zloboha's arm and led her away.

He went with her to her chamber where she had the golden spinning wheel and she took it out and showed it to him. Dobromil admired it greatly.

"Sit down, Dobrunka," he said, "and spin. I should like to see you again at the distaff."

Zloboha at once sat down behind the wheel. She put her foot to the treadle and started the wheel. Instantly the wheel sang out and this is what it sang:

> *"Master, master, don't believe her!*
> *She's a cruel and base deceiver!*
> *She is not your own sweet wife!*
> *She destroyed Dobrunka's life!"*

Zloboha sat stunned and motionless while the king looked wildly about to see where the song came from.

When he could see nothing, he told her to spin some more. Trembling, she obeyed. Hardly had she put her foot to the treadle when the voice again sang out:

> "*Master, master, don't believe her!*
> *She's a cruel and base deceiver!*
> *She has killed her sister good*
> *And hid her body in the wood!*"

Beside herself with fright, Zloboha wanted to flee the spinning wheel, but Dobromil restrained her. Suddenly her face grew so hideous with fear that Dobromil saw she was not his own gentle Dobrunka. With a rough hand he forced her back to the stool and in a stern voice ordered her to spin.

Again she turned the fatal wheel and then for the third time the voice sang out:

> "*Master, master, haste away!*
> *To the wood without delay!*
> *In a cave your wife, restored,*
> *Yearns for you, her own true lord!*"

At those words Dobromil released Zloboha and ran like mad out of the chamber and down into the courtyard where he ordered his swiftest horse to be saddled instantly. The attendants, frightened by his appearance, lost no time and almost at once Dobromil was on his horse and flying over hill and dale so fast that the horse's hoofs scarcely touched the earth.

When he reached the forest he did not know where to look for the cave. He rode straight into the wood until a white doe crossed his path. Then the horse in fright plunged to one side and pushed through bushes and undergrowth to the base of a big rock. Dobromil dismounted and tied the horse to a tree.

He climbed the rock and there he saw something white gleaming among the trees. He crept forward cautiously and suddenly found himself in front of a cave. Imagine then his joy, when he enters and finds his own dear wife Dobrunka.

As he kisses her and looks into her sweet gentle face he says: "Where were my eyes that I was deceived for an instant by your wicked sister?"

"What have you heard about my sister?" asked Dobrunka, who as yet knew nothing of the magic spinning wheel.

So the king told her all that had happened and she in turn told him what had befallen her.

"And from the time the hermit disappeared," she

said in conclusion, " the little boy has brought me food every day."

They sat down on the grass and together they ate some fruit from the wooden plate. When they rose to go they took the wooden plate and the cup away with them as keepsakes.

Dobromil seated his wife in front of him on the horse and sped homewards with her. All his people were at the palace gate waiting to tell him what had happened in his absence.

It seems that the devil himself had come and before their very eyes had carried off his wife and mother-in-law. They looked at each other in amazement as Dobromil rode up with what seemed to be the same wife whom the devil had so recently carried off.

Dobromil explained to them what had happened and with one voice they called down punishment on the head of the wicked sister.

The golden spinning wheel had vanished. So Dobrunka hunted out her old one and set to work at once to spin for her husband's shirts. No one in the kingdom had such fine shirts as Dobromil and no one was happier.

THE GOLDEN GODMOTHER

THE STORY OF POOR LUKAS

THE GOLDEN GODMOTHER

THERE was once a wealthy farmer named Lukas who was so careless in the management of his affairs that there came a time when all his property was gone and he had nothing left but one old tumble-down cottage. Then when it was too late he realized how foolish he had been.

He had always prayed for a child but during the years of his prosperity God had never heard him. Now when he was so poor that he had nothing to eat, his wife gave birth to a little daughter. He looked at the poor unwelcome little stranger and sighed, for he didn't know how he was going to take care of it.

The first thing to be thought about was the christening. Lukas went to the wife of a laborer who lived nearby and asked her to be godmother. She refused because she didn't see that it would do her any good to be godmother to a child of a man as poor as Lukas.

" You see, Lukas, what happens to a man who has

wasted his property," his wife said. "While we were rich the burgomaster himself was our friend, but now even that poverty-stricken woman won't raise a finger to help us. . . . See how the poor infant shivers, for I haven't even any old rags in which to wrap it! And it has to lie on the bare straw! God have mercy on us, how poor we are!" So she wept over the baby, covering it with tears and kisses.

Suddenly a happy thought came to her. She wiped away her tears and said to her husband:

"I beg you, Lukas, go to our old neighbor, the burgomaster's wife. She is wealthy. I'm sure she hasn't forgotten that I was godmother to her child. Go and ask her if she will be godmother to mine."

"I don't think she will," Lukas answered, "but I'll ask her."

With a heavy heart he went by the fields and the barns that had once been his own and entered the house of his old friend, the burgomaster.

"God bless you, neighbor," he said to the burgomaster's wife. "My wife sends her greeting and bids me tell you that God has given us a little daughter whom she wants you to hold at the christening."

The burgomaster's wife looked at him and laughed in his face.

"My dear Lukas, of course I should like to do this for you, but times are hard. Nowadays a person needs every penny and it would take a good deal to help such poor beggars as you. Why don't you ask some one else? Why have you picked me out?"

"Because my wife was godmother to your child."

"Oh, that's it, is it? What you did for me at that time was a loan, was it? And now you want me to give you back as much as you gave me, eh? I'll do no such thing! If I were as generous as you used to be, I'd soon go the way you have gone. No! I shall not walk one step toward that christening!"

Without answering her, Lukas turned and went home in tears.

"You see, dear wife," he said when he got there, "it turned out as I knew it would. But don't be discouraged, for God never entirely forsakes any one. Give me the child and I myself will carry it to the christening and the first person I meet I shall take for godmother."

Weeping all the while, the wife wrapped the baby in a piece of old skirt and placed it in her husband's arms.

On the way to the chapel, Lukas came to a crossroads where he met an old woman.

"Grandmother," he said, "will you be godmother to my child?" And he explained to her how every one else had refused on account of his poverty and how in desperation he had decided to ask the first person he met. "And so, dear grandmother," he concluded, "I am asking you."

"Of course I'll be godmother," the old woman said. "Here, give me the dear wee thing!"

So Lukas gave her the child and together they went on to the chapel.

As they arrived the priest was just ready to leave. The sexton hurried up to him and whispered that a christening party was coming.

"Who is it?" he asked, impatiently.

"Oh, it's only that good-for-nothing of a Lukas who is poorer than a church mouse."

The godmother saw that the sexton was whispering something unfriendly, so she pulled out a shining ducat from her pocket, stepped up to the priest, and pressed it into his hand.

The priest blinked his eyes in amazement, looking first at the ducat and then at the shabby old woman who had given it. He stuffed the ducat into his pocket, whispered hurriedly to the sexton to bring him the font, and then christened the child of poor Lukas with as much ceremony as the child of the richest townsman. The little girl received the name Marishka.

After the christening the priest accompanied the godmother to the door of the chapel and the sexton went even farther until he, too, received the reward for which he was hoping.

When Lukas and the old woman came to the crossroads where they had met, she handed him the child. Then she reached into her pocket, drew out another golden ducat which she stuck into a fold of the child's clothes, and said: " From this ducat with which I endow my godchild, you will have enough to bring her up properly. She will always be a joy and a comfort to you, and when she grows up she will make a happy marriage. Now good-by."

She drew a green wand from her bosom and touched the earth. Instantly a lovely rosebush appeared, covered with blooms. At the same moment the old woman vanished.

In bewilderment Lukas looked this way and that but she was gone. He was so surprised that he didn't know what had happened. I really think he would be standing on that same spot to this day if little Marishka had not begun to cry and by this reminded him of home.

His wife, meantime, was anxiously awaiting him. She, poor soul, was suffering the pangs of hunger, thirst, and bodily pain. There wasn't a mouthful of bread in the house, nor a cent of money.

As Lukas entered the room, he said: "Weep no more, dear wife. Here is your little Marishka. But before you kiss the child, take out the christening gift that you will find tucked away in her clothes. From it you will know what an excellent godmother she has."

The wife reached into the clothes and pulled out not one ducat but a whole handful of ducats!

"Oh!" she gasped and in her surprise she dropped the ducats and they rolled about in the straw that littered the wretched floor.

"Husband! Husband! Who gave you so much money? Just look!"

"I have already looked and at first when I saw them I was more surprised than you are. Now let me tell you where they come from."

So Lukas related to his wife all that had happened at the christening. In conclusion he said: "When I saw the old woman was really gone, I started home. On the way curiosity overcame me and I drew out the christening present and instead of one ducat I found a handful. I can tell you I was surprised but instead of letting them drop on the ground I let them slip back into the baby's clothes. I said to myself: 'Let your wife also have the pleasure of pulling out those golden horses.' And now, dear wife, leave off exclaiming. Give thanks to God for that which he has bestowed upon us and help me gather up the golden darlings, for we don't want any one coming in and spying on us just now."

As they began picking them up, they had a new surprise. Wherever there was one ducat, there they found ten! When they got them all together they made a fine big heap.

"Oh, dear, oh, dear!" said the woman as she gazed at the pile. "Who knows whether this money will be blessed to our use? Perhaps that old woman was an evil spirit who just wants to buy our souls!"

Lukas looked at his wife reprovingly. "How can you be so foolish? Do you suppose an evil spirit would have gone with me to church, allowed herself to be sprinkled with holy water, yes, and even herself make the sign of the cross! Never! I don't say that she is just an ordinary human being, but I do say that she must be a good spirit whom God has sent to us to help us. I'm sure we can keep this money with a clear conscience. The first question is where to hide it so that no one can find it. For the present I shall put it into the chest, but tomorrow night I shall bury it under the pear tree. And one thing, wife, I warn you: don't say anything about it to any one. I shall take one ducat and go to the burgomaster's wife and ask her to change it. Then I shall go buy some milk and eggs and bread and flour, and I'll bring back a woman with me who will make us a fine supper. Tomorrow I'll go to town and buy some clothes and feather beds. After that what else shall I buy? Can you guess?"

"The best thing to do would be to buy back our old property—the house, the fields, and the live stock, and then manage it more wisely than before."

"You're right, wife, that's just what I'll do. And I will manage prudently this time! I have learned my lesson, I can tell you, for poverty is a good teacher."

When Lukas had hidden the money in the chest and turned the key, he took one ducat and went out to make his purchases. While he was gone his wife spent the time nursing the child and weaving happy dreams that now, she was sure, would come to pass.

After a short hour the door opened and Lukas and

a red-cheeked maid entered. The maid carried a great pail of foaming milk. Lukas followed her with a basket of eggs in one hand and on top of the eggs two big round brown cakes, and in the other hand a load of feather beds tied in a knot.

" God be with you! " said the maid, placing the milk pail on the bench. " My mistress, the burgomaster's wife, greets you and sends you some milk for pudding. If there is anything else you need you are to let her know." The maid curtsied and went away before the poor woman could express her thanks.

Lukas laughed and said: " You see, wife, what just one ducat did! If they knew how many more we had they would carry us about in their arms! The burgomaster's wife has sent us all these things. She is lending us feather beds until tomorrow and she is going to send us an old woman to help us out. I told her our child had received a handful of ducats as a christening gift. If she comes here to see you, make up your mind what you're going to say."

Then Lukas built a fire. Presently the old woman came and soon good hot soup was ready. It was just plain milk soup, but I can tell you it tasted better to hungry Lukas and his wife than the rich food which the king himself ate that day from a golden platter.

The next day after breakfast Lukas set out for town. The burgomaster's wife took advantage of his absence to visit his wife and find out what she could about the money.

" My dear neighbor," she said, after she had made the necessary inquiries about health, " the blessing of God came into your house with that child."

" Oh," said the other, " if you mean the christening gift, it isn't so very much. A handful of ducats soon roll away. However, may God repay that good woman, the godmother. At least we can now buy back our old farm and live like respectable people."

On the way home the burgomaster's wife stopped at the houses of her various friends and gave them a full account of Lukas' wealth. Before noon every small boy in the village knew that at Lukas' house they had a hogshead of ducats.

In the evening Lukas came back from town driving a cart that was piled high with furniture and clothing and feather beds and food. The next day he bought back his old farm with the cattle and the implements.

This marked the beginning of a new life for Lukas. He set to work with industry and put into practice all the lessons that poverty had taught him.

He and his wife lived happily. Their greatest joy

was Marishka, a little girl so charming and so pretty that every one loved her on sight.

" Dear neighbor," all the old women used to say to the child's mother, " that girl of yours will never grow up. She's far too wise for her years! "

But Marishka did very well. She grew up into a beautiful young woman and one day a prince saw her, fell in love with her, and married her. So the old godmother's prophecy that Marishka would make a happy marriage was fulfilled.

THE GOLDEN DUCK

THE STORY OF PRINCE RADUZ
AND THE FAITHFUL LUDMILA

THE GOLDEN DUCK

O NCE upon a time there was a king who had four
sons. One day the queen said to him:

" It is time that one of our boys went out into the
world to make his fortune."

" I have been thinking that very same thing," the
king said. " Let us get ready Raduz, our youngest,
and send him off with God's blessing."

Preparations were at once made and in a
few days Raduz bid his parents farewell and set
forth.

He traveled many days and many nights over
desert plains and through dense forests until he came
to a high mountain. Halfway up the mountain he
found a house.

" I'll stop here," he thought to himself, " and see
if they'll take me into service."

Now this house was occupied by three people: old
Yezibaba, who was a bad old witch; her husband, who
was a wizard but not so bad as Yezibaba; and their

daughter, Ludmila, the sweetest, kindest girl that two wicked parents ever had.

"Good day to you all," Raduz said, as he stepped into the house and bowed.

"The same to you," old Yezibaba answered. "What brings you here?"

"I'm looking for work and I thought you might have something for me to do."

"What can you do?" Yezibaba asked.

"I'll do anything you set me to. I'm trustworthy and industrious."

Yezibaba didn't want to take him, but the old man wanted him and in the end Yezibaba with very ill grace consented to give him a trial.

He rested that night and early next morning presented himself to the old witch and said:

"What work am I to do today, mistress?"

Yezibaba looked him over from head to foot. Then she took him to a window and said: "What do you see out there?"

"I see a rocky hillside."

"Good. Go to that rocky hillside, cultivate it, plant it in trees that will grow, blossom, and bear fruit tonight. Tomorrow morning bring me the ripe fruit. Here is a wooden hoe with which to work."

"Alas," thought Raduz to himself, "did ever a man have such a task as this? What can I do on that rocky hillside with a wooden hoe? How can I finish my task in so short a time?"

He started to work but he hadn't struck three blows with the wooden hoe before it broke. In despair he tossed it aside and sat down under a beech tree.

In the meantime wicked old Yezibaba had cooked a disgusting mess of toads which she told Ludmila to carry out to the serving man for his dinner. Ludmila was sorry for the poor young man who had fallen into her mother's clutches and she said to herself: "What has he done to deserve such unkind treatment? I won't let him eat this nasty mess. I'll share my own dinner with him."

She waited until her mother was out of the room, then she took Yezibaba's magic wand and hid it under her apron. After that she hurried out to Raduz, whom she found sitting under the beech tree with his face in his hands.

"Don't be discouraged," she said to him. "It is true your mistress cooked you a mess of toads for your dinner but, see, I have thrown them away and have brought you my own dinner instead. As for your task," she continued, "I will help you with that. Here is my mother's magic wand. I have but to strike the rocky hillside and by tomorrow the trees that my mother has ordered will spring up, blossom, and bear fruit."

Ludmila did as she promised. She struck the ground with the magic wand and instantly instead of the rocky hillside there appeared an orchard with rows on rows of trees that blossomed and bore fruit as you watched them.

Raduz looked from Ludmila to the orchard and couldn't find words with which to express his surprise and gratitude. Then Ludmila spread out her dinner and together they ate it, laughing merrily and talking. Raduz would have kept Ludmila all the afternoon but she remembered that Yezibaba was waiting for her and she hurried away.

The next morning Raduz presented Yezibaba a basket of ripe fruit. She sniffed it suspiciously and then very grudgingly acknowledged that he had accomplished his task.

" What am I to do today? " Raduz asked.

Yezibaba led him to a second window and asked him what he saw there.

" I see a rocky ravine covered with brambles," he said.

"Right. Go now and clear away the brambles, dig up the ravine, and plant it in grape vines. Tomorrow morning bring me the ripe grapes. Here is another wooden hoe with which to work."

Raduz took the hoe and set to work manfully. At the first blow the hoe broke into three pieces.

"Alas," he thought, "what is going to happen to me now? Unless Ludmila helps me again, I am lost."

At home Yezibaba was busy cooking a mess of serpents. When noonday came she said to Ludmila: "Here, my child, is dinner for the serving man. Take it out to him."

Ludmila took the nasty mess and, as on the day before, threw it away. Then again hiding Yezibaba's wand under her apron, she went to Raduz, carrying in her hands her own dinner.

Raduz saw her coming and at once his heart grew light and he thought to himself how kind Ludmila was and how beautiful.

"I have been sitting here idle," he told her, "for at the first blow my hoe broke. Unless you help me, I don't know what I shall do."

"Don't worry," Ludmila said. "It is true your mistress sent you a mess of serpents for your dinner, but I threw them out and have brought you my own dinner instead. And I've brought the magic wand, too, so it will be easy enough to plant a vineyard that will produce ripe grapes by tomorrow morning."

They ate together and after dinner Ludmila took the wand and struck the earth. At once a vineyard appeared and, as they watched, the vines blossomed and the blooms turned to grapes.

It was harder than before for Raduz to let Ludmila go, for he wanted to keep on talking to her forever, but she remembered that Yezibaba was waiting for her and she hurried away.

The next morning when Raduz presented a basket of ripe grapes, old Yezibaba could scarcely believe her eyes. She sniffed the grapes suspiciously and then very grudgingly acknowledged that he had accomplished his second task.

"What am I to do today?" Raduz asked.

Yezibaba led him to a third window and told him to look out and tell her what he saw.

"I see a great rocky cliff."

"Right," she said. "Go now to that cliff and grind me flour out of the rocks and from the flour bake me bread. Tomorrow morning bring me the fresh loaves. Today you shall have no tools of any kind. Go now and do this task or suffer the consequences."

As Raduz started off, Yezibaba looked after him and shook her head suspiciously.

" I don't understand this," she said to her husband. " He could never have done these two tasks alone. Do you suppose Ludmila has been helping him? I'll punish her if she has! "

" Shame on you," the old man said, " to talk so of your own daughter! Ludmila is a good girl and has always been loyal and obedient."

" I hope so," Yezibaba said, " but just the same I think I myself will carry him out his dinner today."

" Nonsense, old woman! You'll do no such thing! You're always smelling a rat somewhere! Let the boy alone and don't go nagging at Ludmila either! "

So Yezibaba said no more. This time she cooked a mess of lizards for Raduz' dinner.

" Here, Ludmila," she said, " carry this out to the young man. But see that you don't talk to him. And hurry back."

Poor Raduz had been pounding stones one on another as well as he could, but he hadn't been able to grind any of them into flour. As noonday approached he kept looking up anxiously to see whether beautiful Ludmila was again coming to help him.

" Here I am," she called while she was yet some

distance away. "You were to have lizard stew today but, see, I am bringing you my own dinner!"

Then she told him what she had heard Yezibaba say to her father.

"Today she almost brought you your dinner herself, for she suspects that I have been helping you. If she knew that I really had she would kill you."

"Dear Ludmila," Raduz said, "I know very well that without you I am lost! How can I ever thank you for all you have done for me?"

Ludmila said she didn't want thanks. She was helping Raduz because she was sorry for him and loved him.

Then she took Yezibaba's wand and struck the rocky cliff. At once, instead of the bare rock, there were sacks of grain and a millstone that worked merrily away grinding out fine flour. As you watched, the flour was kneaded up into loaves and then, pop went the loaves into a hot oven and soon the air was sweet with the smell of baking bread.

Raduz begged Ludmila to stay and talk to him, but she remembered that the old witch was waiting for her and she hurried home.

The next morning Raduz carried the baked loaves to Yezibaba. She sniffed at them suspiciously and then her wicked heart nearly cracked with bitterness to think that Raduz had accomplished his third task. But she hid her disappointment and pretending to smile, she said:

" I see, my dear boy, that you have been able to do all the tasks that I have set you. This is enough for the present. Today you may rest."

That night the old witch hatched the plot of boiling Raduz alive. She had him fill a big cauldron with water and put it on the fire. Then she said to her husband:

" Now, old man, I'm going to take a nap but when the water boils wake me up."

As soon as Yezibaba was asleep Ludmila gave the old man strong wine until he, too, fell asleep. Then she called Raduz and told him what Yezibaba was planning to do.

" You must escape while you can," she said, " for if you are here tomorrow you will surely be thrown into the boiling cauldron."

But Raduz had fallen too deeply in love with Ludmila to leave her and now he declared that he would never go unless she went with him.

" Very well," Ludmila said, " I will go with you if you swear you will never forget me."

"Forget you? How could I forget you," Raduz said, "when I wouldn't give you up for the whole world!"

So Raduz took a solemn oath and they made ready to flee. Ludmila threw down her kerchief in one corner of the house and Raduz' cap in another. Then she took Yezibaba's wand and off they started.

The next morning when the old man awoke, he called out: "Hi, there, boy! Are you still asleep?"

"No, I'm not asleep," answered Raduz' cap. "I'm just stretching."

Presently the old man called out again: "Here, boy, hand me my clothes."

"In a minute," the cap answered. "Just wait till I put on my slippers."

Then old Yezibaba awoke. "Ludmila!" she cried. "Get up, you lazy girl, and hand me my skirt and bodice."

"In a minute! In a minute!" the kerchief answered.

"What's the matter?" Yezibaba scolded. "Why are you so long dressing?"

"Just one more minute!" the kerchief said.

But Yezibaba, who was an impatient old witch, sat up in bed and then she could see that Ludmila's bed was empty. That threw her into a fine rage and she called out to her husband:

"Now, old man, what have you got to say? As sure as I'm alive that good-for-nothing boy is gone and that precious daughter of yours has gone with him!"

"No, no," the old man said. "I don't think so."

Then they both got up and sure enough neither Raduz nor Ludmila was to be found.

"What do you think now, you old booby!" Yezibaba shouted. "A mighty good and loyal and obedient girl that daughter of yours is! But why do you stand there all day? Mount the black steed and fly after them and when you overtake them bring them back to me and I'll punish them properly!"

In the meantime Raduz and Ludmila were fleeing as fast as they could.

Suddenly Ludmila said: "Oh, how my left cheek burns! I wonder what it means? Look back, dear Raduz, and see if there is any one following us."

Raduz turned and looked. "There's nothing following us," he said, "but a black cloud in the sky."

"A black cloud? That's the old man on the black horse that rides on the clouds. Quick! We must be ready for him!"

Ludmila struck the ground with Yezibaba's wand

and changed it into a field. She turned herself into the growing rye and made Raduz the reaper who was cutting the rye. Then she instructed him how to answer the old man with cunning.

The black cloud descended upon them with thunder and a shower of hailstones that beat down the growing rye.

"Take care!" Raduz cried. "You're trampling my rye! Leave some of it for me."

"Very well," the old man said, alighting from his steed, "I'll leave some of it for you. But tell me, reaper, have you seen anything of two young people passing this way?"

"Not a soul has passed while I've been reaping, but I do remember that while I was planting this field two such people did pass."

The old man shook his head, mounted his steed, and flew home again on the black cloud.

"Well, old wiseacre," said Yezibaba, "what brings you back so soon?"

"No use my going on," the old man said. "The only person I saw was a reaper in a field of rye."

"You booby!" cried Yezibaba, "not to know that Raduz was the reaper and Ludmila the rye! How they fooled you! And didn't you bring me back just one stalk of rye? Go after them again and this time don't let them fool you!"

In the meantime Raduz and Ludmila were hurrying on. Suddenly Ludmila said:

"I wonder why my left cheek burns? Look back, dear Raduz, and see if there is any one following us."

Raduz turned and looked. "There's nothing following us but a gray cloud in the sky."

"A gray cloud? That's the old man on the gray horse that rides on the clouds. But don't be afraid. Only have ready a cunning answer."

Ludmila struck her hat with the wand and changed it into a chapel. Herself she changed into a fly that attracted a host of other flies. She changed Raduz into a hermit. All the flies flew into the chapel and Raduz began preaching to them.

Suddenly the gray cloud descended on the chapel with a flurry of snow and such cold that the shingles of the roof crackled.

The old man alighted from the gray steed and entered the chapel.

"Hermit," he said to Raduz, "have you seen two travelers go by here, a girl and a youth?"

"As long as I've been preaching here," Raduz said, "I've had only flies for a congregation. But I do remember that while the chapel was building two such people did go by. But now I must beg you, good sir, to go out, for you are letting in so much cold that my congregation is freezing."

At that the old man mounted his steed and flew back home on the gray cloud.

Old Yezibaba was waiting for him. When she saw him coming she called out:

"Again you bring no one, you good-for-nothing! Where did you leave them this time?" .

"Where did I leave them?" the old man said. "How could I leave them when I didn't even see them? All I saw was a little chapel and a hermit preaching to a congregation of flies. I almost froze the congregation to death!"

"Oh, what a booby you are!" Yezibaba cried. "Raduz was the hermit and Ludmila one of the flies! Why didn't you bring me just one shingle from the roof of the chapel? I see I'll have to go after them myself!"

In a rage she mounted the third magic steed and flew off.

In the meantime Raduz and Ludmila were hurrying on. Suddenly Ludmila said:

"I wonder why my left cheek burns? Look back,

dear Raduz, again, and see if there is any one following us."

Raduz turned and looked. " There's nothing following us but a red cloud in the sky."

" A red cloud? That must be Yezibaba herself on the steed of fire. Now indeed we must be careful. Up to this it has been easy enough but it won't be easy to deceive her. Here we are beside a lake. I will change myself into a golden duck and float on the water. Do you dive into the water so that she can't burn you. When she alights and tries to catch me, do you jump up and get the horse by the bridle. Don't be afraid at what will happen."

The fiery cloud descended, burning up everything it touched. At the edge of the water Yezibaba alighted from her steed and tried to catch the golden duck. The duck fluttered on and on just out of her reach and Yezibaba went farther and farther from her horse.

Then Raduz leaped out of the water and caught the horse by its bridle. At once the duck rose on its wings and flew to Raduz and became again Ludmila. Together they mounted the fiery steed and flew off over the lake.

Yezibaba, helpless with rage and dismay, called after them a bitter curse:

"If you, Raduz, are kissed by woman before you wed Ludmila, then will you forget Ludmila! And you, ungrateful girl, if once Raduz forgets you then he shall not remember you again until seven long years have come and gone!"

Raduz and Ludmila rode on and on until they neared Raduz' native city. There they met a man of whom Raduz asked the news.

"News indeed!" the man said. "The king and his three older sons are dead. Only the queen is alive and she cries night and day for her youngest son who went out into the world and has never been heard of since. The whole city is in an uproar as to who shall be the new king."

When Raduz heard this he said to Ludmila: "Do you, my dear Ludmila, wait for me here outside the city while I go quickly to the palace and let it be known that I am alive and am returned. It would not be fitting to present you to my mother, the queen, in those ragged clothes. As soon as I am made king I shall come for you, bringing you a beautiful dress."

Ludmila agreed to this and Raduz left her and hurried to the castle. His mother recognized him at once and ran with open arms to greet him. She wanted to kiss him but he wouldn't let her. The news of his return flew abroad and he was immediately proclaimed king. A great feast was spread and all the people ate and drank and made merry.

Fatigued with his journey and with the excitement of his return, Raduz lay down to rest. While he slept his mother came in and kissed him on both cheeks. Instantly Yezibaba's curse was fulfilled and all memory of Ludmila left him.

Poor Ludmila waited for his return but he never came. Then she knew what must have happened. Heartbroken and lonely she found a spot near a farmhouse that commanded a view of the castle, and she stood there day after day hoping to see Raduz. She stood there so long that finally she took root and grew up into a poplar tree that was so beautiful that soon throughout the countryside people began talking about it. Every one admired it but the young king. He when he looked at it always felt unhappy and he supposed this was because it obstructed the view from his window. At last he ordered it to be cut down.

The farmer near whose house it stood begged hard to have it saved, but the king was firm.

Shortly after the poplar was cut down there grew up under the king's very window a pretty little pear tree that bore golden pears. It was a wonderful little tree. No matter how many pears you picked in the evening, by the next morning the tree would again be full.

The king loved the little tree and was forever talking about it. The old queen, on the other hand, disliked it.

" I wish that tree would die," she used to say. " There's something strange about it that makes me nervous."

The king begged her to leave the tree alone but she worried and complained and nagged until at last for his own peace of mind he had the poor little pear tree cut down.

The seven years of Yezibaba's curse at last ran out. Then Ludmila changed herself again into a little golden duck and went swimming about on the lake that was under the king's window.

Suddenly the king began to remember that he had seen that duck before. He ordered it to be caught and brought to him. But none of his people could catch it. Then he called together all the fishermen and birdcatchers in the country but none of them could catch the strange duck.

The days went by and the king's mind was more and more engrossed with the thought of the golden duck. "If no one can catch it for me," he said at last, "I must try to catch it myself."

So he went to the lake and reached out his hand after the golden duck. The duck led him on and on but at last she allowed herself to be caught. As soon as she was in his hand she changed to herself and Raduz recognized her as his own beautiful Ludmila.

She said to him: "I have been true to you but you have forgotten me all these years. Yet I forgive you, for it was not your fault."

In Raduz' heart his old love returned a hundred-fold and he was overjoyed to lead Ludmila to the castle. He presented her to his mother and said:

"This is she who saved my life many times. She and no one else will be my wife."

A great wedding feast was prepared and so at last Raduz married the faithful Ludmila.

THE STORY THAT NEVER ENDS

THE STORY THAT NEVER ENDS

(To be told very seriously)

ONCE upon a time there was a shepherd who had a great flock of sheep. He used to pasture them in a meadow on the other side of a brook. One day the sun had already set before he started home. Recent rains had swollen the brook so that he and the sheep had to cross on a little footbridge. The bridge was so narrow that the sheep had to pass over one by one.

Now we'll wait until he drives them all over. Then I'll go on with my story.

(When the children grow impatient and beg for a continuation of the story, they are told that there are many sheep and that up to this time only a few have crossed. A little later when their impatience again breaks out, they are told that the sheep are still crossing. And so on indefinitely. In conclusion:)

In fact there were so many sheep that when morning came they were still crossing, and then it was time for the shepherd to turn around and drive them back again to pasture!

Other titles from
THE HIPPOCRENE LIBRARY
OF FOLKLORE...

Fairy Gold: A Book of Classic English Fairy Tales
Chosen by Ernest Rhys
Illustrated by Herbert Cole
"The Fairyland which you enter, through the golden door of this book, is pictured in tales and rhymes that have been told at one time or another to English children," begins this charming volume of favorite English fairy tales. Forty-nine imaginative black and white illustrations accompany thirty classic tales, including such beloved stories as "Jack and the Bean Stalk," "The Three Bears," and "Chicken Licken" (Chicken Little to American audiences). *Ages 9-12*
236 pages • 5 1/2 x 8 1/4 • 49 b/w illustrations • 0-7818-0700-X • W • $14.95hc • (790)

Folk Tales from Bohemia
Adolf Wenig
This folk tale collection is one of a kind, focusing uniquely on humankind's struggle with evil in the world. Delicately ornate red and black text and illustrations set the mood. "How the Devil Contended with Man," "The Devil's Gifts," and "How an Old Woman Cheated the Devil" are just 2 of 9 suspenseful folk tales which interweave good and evil, magic and reality, struggle and conquest. *Ages 9 -12*
98 pages • red and black illustrations • 5 1/2 x 8 1/4 • 0-7818-0718-2 • W • $14.95hc • (786)

Folk Tales from Chile
Brenda Hughes

This selection of 15 tales gives a taste of the variety of Chile's rich folklore. There is a story of the spirit who lived in a volcano and kept his daughter imprisoned in the mountain, guarded by a devoted dwarf; there are domestic tales with luck favoring the poor and simple, and tales which tell how poppies first appeared in the cornfields and how the Big Stone in Lake Llanquihue came to be there. Fifteen charming illustrations accompany the text. *Ages 7-10*

121 pages • 5 1/2 x 8 1/4 • 15 illustrations • 0-7818-0712-3 • W • $12.50hc • (785)

Folk Tales from Russia
by Donald A. Mackenzie

From Hippocrene's classic folklore series comes this collection of short stories of myth, fable, and adventure—all infused with the rich and varied cultural identity of Russia. With nearly 200 pages and 8 full-page black-and-white illustrations, the reader will be charmed by these legendary folk tales that symbolically weave magical fantasy with the historic events of Russia's past. *Ages 9-12*

192 pages • 8 b/w illustrations • 5 1/2 x 8 1/4 • 0-7818-0696-8 • W• $12.50hc • (788)

Folk Tales from Simla

Alice Elizabeth Dracott

From Simla, once the summer capital of India under British rule, comes a charming collection of Himalayan folk lore, known for its beauty, wit, and mysticism. These 56 stories, fire-side tales of the hill-folk of Northern India, will surely delight readers of all ages. Eight illustrations by the author complete this delightful volume. *Ages 12 and up*

225 pages • 5 1/2 x 8 1/4 • 8 illustrations • 0-7818-0704-2 • W • $14.95hc • (794)

Folk Tales from Turkey

Collected by Dr. Ignacz Kunos, translated by R. Nisbet, illustrated by Celia Levetus

These 17 classic Turkish folk tales whisk the reader into a realm of romance, iniquity, suspense, and adventure. "The Piece of Liver," "The Rose-Beauty," and "The Ghost of the Spring and the Shrew," are just a few examples of the folk tales presented in this collection—each story uniquely weaving the important threads of Turkish customs, culture, and values with magic and fantasy, deeply rooted in Turkish tradition. Seven beautiful black-and-white line drawings bring these stories to life. *Ages 12 and up*

205 pages • 7 b/w line drawings • 5 1/2 x 8 1/4 • 0-7818-0697-6 • W• $14.95hc • (795)

Glass Mountain: Twenty-Eight Ancient Polish Folk Tales and Fables

W.S. Kuniczak

Illustrated by Pat Bargielski

As a child in a far-away misty corner of Volhynia, W.S. Kuniczak was carried away to an extraordinary world of magic and illusion by the folk tales of his Polish nurse. "To this day I merely need to close my eyes to see . . . an imaginary picture show and chart the marvelous geography of the fantastic," he writes in his introduction.

171 pages • 6 x 9 • 8 illustrations • 0-7818-0552-X • W • $16.95hc • (645)

The Little Mermaid and Other Tales

Hans Christian Andersen

Here is a near replica of the first American edition of 27 classic fairy tales from the masterful Hans Christian Andersen. Children and adults alike will enjoy timeless favorites including "The Little Mermaid," "The Emperor's New Clothes," "The Little Matchgirl," and "The Ugly Duckling." These stories, and many more, whisk the reader to magical lands, fantastic voyages, romantic encounters, and suspenseful adventures. Beautiful black-and-white sketches enhance these fairy tales and bring them to life.

Ages 9-12

508 pages • color, b/w illustrations • 6 1/8 x 9 1/4 • 0-7818-0720-4 • W • $19.95hc • (791)

Old Polish Legends

Retold by F.C. Anstruther

Wood engravings by J. Sekalski

Now available in a new gift edition! This fine collection of eleven fairy tales, with an introduction by Zymunt Nowakowski, was first published in Scotland during World War II, when the long night of the German occupation was at its darkest. The tales, however, "recall the ancient beautiful times, to laugh and to weep . . ."

66 pages • 7 1/4 x 9 • 11 woodcut engravings • 0-78180521-X • W • $11.95hc • (653)

Pakistani Folk Tales: Toontoony Pie and Other Stories

Ashraf Siddiqui and Marilyn Lerch

Illustrated by Jan Fairservis

In this collection of 22 folk tales set in the regions of Punjab and Bengal that now comprise Pakistan, are found not only the familiar figures of folklore—kings and beautiful princesses—but the magic of the Far East, cunning jackals, and wise holy men. Thirty-eight charming illustrations by Jan Fairservis complete this enchanting collection. *Ages 7-10*

158 pages • 6 x 9 • 38 illustrations • 0-7818-0703-4 • W • $12.50hc • (784)

Polish Fables: Bilingual Edition
Ignacy Krasicki
Translated by Gerard T. Kapolka
Ignacy Krasicki (1735-1801) was hailed as "The Prince of Poets" by his contemporaries. With great artistry the author used contemporary events and human relations to show a course to guide human conduct. For over two centuries, Krasicki's fables have entertained and instructed his delighted readers. This bilingual gift edition contains the original Polish text with side-by side English translation. Twenty illustrations by Barbara Swidzinska , a well known Polish artist, add to the volume's charm.
105 pages • 6 x 9 • 20 illustrations • 0-7818-0548-1 • W • $19.95hc • (646)

Swedish Fairy Tales
Translated by H. L. Braekstad
A unique blending of enchantment, adventure, comedy, and romance make this collection of Swedish fairy tales a must-have for any library. With 18 different, classic Swedish fairy tales and 21 beautiful black-and-white illustrations, this is an ideal gift for children and adults alike. *Ages 9-12*
190 pages • 21 b/w illustrations • 5 1/2 x 81/4 • 0-7818-0717-4 • W • $12.50hc • (787)

Tales of Languedoc: From the South of France
Samuel Jacques Brun

For children to older adults (and everyone in between), here is a masterful collection of folktales from the South of France. Thirty-three beautiful black-and-white illustrations throughout bring magic, life, and spirit to such classic French folk tales as "My Grandfather's Tour of France," "A Blind Man's Story," and "The Marriage of Monsieur Arcanvel." Travel to ancient castles, villages, and countrysides, and experience the romance and adventure in these nine stories. *Ages 12 and up*
248 pages • 33 b/w sketches • 5 1/2 x 8 1/4 • 0-7818-0715-8 • W • $14.95 hc • (793)

Twenty Scottish Tales and Legends
Edited by Cyril Swinson
Illustrated by Allan Stewart

Twenty enchanting myths take the reader to an extraordinary world of magic harps, angry giants, mysterious spells and gallant Knights. Amusingly divided into sections such as Tales of Battle and Pursuit, Kings and Conquests, and Tales of Daring, this book brings to life the legendary Scottish mythology of ages past. Eight detailed illustrations by Allan Stewart bring the beauty of the Scottish countryside to the collection. *Ages 9-12*
215 pages • 5 1/2 x 8 1/4 • 8 b/w illustrations • 0-7818-0701-8 • W • $14.95 hc • (789)

All prices subject to change. **To purchase Hippocrene Books** contact your local bookstore, call (718) 454-2366, or write to: HIPPOCRENE BOOKS, 171 Madison Avenue, New York, NY 10016. Please enclose check or money order, adding $5.00 shipping (UPS) for the first book and $.50 for each additional book.